£1.00

Jill Has Two Horses

by Jemma Spark

Epona Publishing

Table of Contents

Chapter One – Typing and Shorthand

At first, I had wanted to call this book *Jill Turns to Crime*, as I thought it would be rather dramatic and eye-catching. I imagined myself in a svelte black leather catsuit, like Honor Blackman in *The Avengers* – although she was a crime-fighter and not the villain! But perhaps you readers might think that such a morally upright young woman as myself would never engage in a criminal act? Even if it did mean making a considerable sum of money to purchase a whizz-bang, stupendous second horse for myself. I nod wisely but loftily declare that I have discovered that as one leaves the schoolroom and ventures into 'real-life', issues once so easily classified as right and wrong become more complex. It is rather like fumbling around in the dark, 'trying to do the right thing'.

It all began with a righteous decision that I should accept an honest job of work that involved a great deal of effort and for which I was to be relatively well paid.

"Jill darling, this is very interesting, just right for you," said Mummy over breakfast at the castle, in a voice that foreshadowed something earth-shattering.

It was the first week in a very cold January in the Scottish Highlands, and we were all tucking into luscious scrambled eggs, bright yellow from the estate's hens, that were looked after by Cook. I found it rather fascinating that Mummy's past obsession with hens, which I considered the most soulless of animals, had been redirected to, of all creatures, sheep! Bonding with Richard, her new husband, she had entered into his delight of the woolly creatures who grazed across the hill slopes that rose above the loch.

"Really," I said, concentrating on my eggs, thinking about my plans for the day to ride my horse, Balius.

"It's from my publisher, and of course, he knows about our situation and your noble attempts to master shorthand and typing," she said wryly.

"What is 'just right' for me?"

"It's a job, helping an old lady to write her memoirs. It involves taking down her dictation in shorthand and typing it up."

I paused with a forkful of egg halfway to my mouth and considered this. It did sound like I was at least somewhat qualified for such a position. I had been typing my own manuscripts since we came to Scotland, and I had been taking shorthand lessons twice a week. I had also been learning German, hoping that one day I might go to Germany as a student in a dressage stable.

"Where is this old lady with the fascinating memories?" I asked.

"Well, therein lies the absolute 'rightness' for you. It is in Cornwall, in a remote house, tucked away in a hidden valley, and you can take your horse with you!" said Mummy with a smug air of having sealed the deal.

"Yes, that does sound fascinating," I commented. Perhaps it was a job uniquely suited to me, as I had been writing my autobiographical pony books for about five years. But, of course, I had worked in all sorts of different jobs over the years as a child, having to make money to keep first one pony, Black Boy, and then later my second pony, Rapide. Now that money was not in short supply, it had become much more complicated, which didn't make sense at all.

Mark Lansdowne, my step-father's spoilt nephew, who I had renamed Malevolent Mark, had accused my mother, behind her back, of being a fortune hunter. This was so not true. Ever since my father died when I was little, Mummy had slaved away writing whimsical children's stories, earning our bread and butter and hay and corn and shoes for my ponies.

She had fallen in love with Richard, who owned Blainstock Castle. It was the love story of the century. So now, Mummy and I slaved away in the summer helping Richard with the guests for the grouse shooting season, and I felt that we were making a meaningful contribution to the estate's business.

Mark avoided us and rarely dined at the castle. He lived next door, on an adjoining estate with his father and mother, Richard's elder sister, Lavinia. Mark was an aspiring three-day event rider, and he kept his horses and trained them at Blainstock stables, attached to the castle owned by Richard. It was a marvellous setup, not only showjumps and two cross-country courses, and a newly built indoor manège. It had all been built at the castle before we had arrived because there had already been stables here, so it seemed simpler to add to them rather than start from scratch at Mark's family estate. It was financed by the joint family trust set up for Richard and his sister.

Now, there was the awkward situation whereby I, as a family member, had use of the stables, and the staff helped me. But Mark was very uppity about it and looked daggers at me as if I was trying to steal his facilities or even his inheritance!

So far, I had edged around Mark, trying to be discreet, riding in the arenas in the middle of the day after he had finished his morning sessions, before he began his afternoon training, avoiding him if I knew he was in the yard.

I admit I was rather fascinated by how he trained his six eventing horses, and sometimes I skulked around corners spying on him. I was particularly intrigued when a shady-looking character turned up three afternoons a week and helped him. On those days, the indoor manège doors were firmly locked on the inside. It was a mystery I was determined to solve one day.

On the rare occasions that Mark dined at the castle, I often made pointed comments about Mummy's successful career as an author. Now the chance for me to earn some money was important in the undeclared battle of who was really taking financial advantage of Richard. This was added to the fact that I was longing for a second horse. I loved Balius, my young Thoroughbred with a dash of Highland pony blood. He had been a gift from Richard. His schooling was coming on well, but I was deliberately taking him very slowly, and I longed for a fully-trained horse that I could forge ahead with now that I was competing in adult classes. My ambition was not just to excel, perhaps one day to 'ride for England' but the rather ignominious goal of beating Mark at his own game. This fierce competition with Mark was the only blight upon our present wonderful situation.

"Yes, that does sound pretty good," I said.

Cornwall was a long way south, and I believed that spring came early there - and the sun shone - for I was growing depressed with the long dark winter up here in Scotland. There seemed to be no bad points with the proposed scheme. I did wonder about this elderly lady and what sort of memoirs she might be writing. Perhaps she had been a war hero working in the French resistance, alluring and adventurous and pulling off dangerous exploits to help Britain win the war. Even better, she might have been an equestrienne of extraordinary ability who had outshone her male counterparts. Or one of the glamorous Bright Young Things getting up to all sorts of amusing mischief.

"Yes, I would like to do it," I said, then wondered whether my shorthand was up to speed. Perhaps I had better do some serious practice. "When would I start?"

"Well, I think I'll ring my publisher, and they can give me the woman's details, and you should write to her, explaining your skills and Balius, and put yourself forward for the position."

This will be one in the eye for Mark, I thought to myself. I hurried down to the stables. During the night, there had been a deep frost, and everything was iced and sparkly. I cut across the courtyard, and my footsteps left marks on the thick, crunchy grass. I strode straight to Balius's stable to wish him good morning. My beautiful horse was tall, 16.2 hh, and a particularly

handsome shade of dapple grey with a flowing white mane and tail. He was very sensible, having inherited the stable temperament of his mother, a darling Highland cross thoroughbred mare called Bonnie. But he also had the speed and strength of his Thoroughbred father, a Premium stallion.

The plan had been that I should break him in myself, but then Mummy and I had gone away to prepare for her wedding. When we had returned, I found that Mark had backed him and ridden him on the tightest of reins, jumped him within a week of backing and done everything the wrong way around. I had spent months retraining him, starting from the beginning. I would never forgive Mark for what he had done. I was utterly implacable on this point. Mark was my mortal enemy.

Balius and I were finally at the stage when we could start jumping in the arena. Today I had a riding lesson booked with Linda, who ran the McNally Riding School two miles beyond the local village. Linda was truly amazing. She had inspired me with the idea of going to a dressage stable in Germany.

Last autumn, she had come first in the open class of the hunter trials that had been held here at Blainstock. Her round had been fast and utterly flawless. Mark had made a big deal of competing *hors concours* – non-competitively - but even if he had been riding seriously to win, I think that Linda would have beaten him. I had left Balius with Linda for a few weeks when I had gone south to my mother's wedding, and she had improved him out of sight. I had had a serious talk with myself about the rights and wrongs of paying someone else to train your horse. I had always prided myself on the fact that I not only cared for my ponies myself but I also trained them. Now I recognised that I would never be the best trainer in the world, and there was no shame or disgrace in paying someone, especially someone as worthy as Linda, to help with the training.

In my lesson today, we began with trotting circles at what she called a working trot. Then we moved on to some lateral work, leg yielding in the circle so that it became smaller and smaller. Then leg yielding back out in the shape of a snail's shell. She suggested we try some different figures, working on a rectangle, leg yielding inwards down the long side to the halfway mark, then back out to the track. Balius felt balanced and obedient, and Linda complimented me on the way that he was going.

"Now I want you to work towards some collection at the canter. You need to ride forwards into collection, don't make the mistake of going backwards."

I was a little puzzled at this. Linda took a breath and tried again.

"You must be riding from the hindleg into the contact, not the other way around. Start with a working canter on the twenty-yard circle. Now we'll

decrease the size of the circle gradually. Ride around twice at sixteen-yards and then twice around at fourteen-yards. Use your inside leg to produce enough impulsion from the hindleg and your outside leg just behind the girth, to help keep Balius on the circle. Make sure you have even contact on the reins, don't try and just turn him with the inside rein. The collection should come to him naturally through his hindquarters on the smaller circle."

This was very hard work. Previously I had thought that sitting in a correct position was the key to good riding. Now I realised that there was much more to it, active riding, not just sitting pretty.

"Right, you've got it. Can you feel it," said Linda.

"Yes, I can!" I was so excited.

"Hold it for one full circle, then let him move back out to a larger circle. As we practise, he should be able to maintain the collection on the larger circle, but it won't come all at once."

"Bring him back to a walk on a loose rein, that's right. Let him relax so that he knows he's done well."

"Now we do it again the other way. Then, we'll go on to jump."

It was amazing how different it felt when I managed to do what Linda was telling me. Then she set up a grid, a row of cavellettis at their lowest height three yards apart. She told me to trot down them. At first, Balius stumbled, put in two strides, hit the poles, then on the third go, he got the idea, and we went beautifully, rounded, bouncing and careful.

"Now, canter!" said Linda.

We cantered, and he did it! He was wonderful!

"I think you've got a natural jumper there!" called Linda.

So far, we had popped over tree trunks lying on the ground and up and down banks, but this was definitely a step up. I loved the feeling of him. He was fantastic! I felt filled with hope that not only would he be a brilliant jumper, but I would be able to train him to get to the top. I was still nervous about open classes and Grade C jumping. All my experience in the under-14s and under-16s seemed like a huge step up.

"What you need is a schoolmaster," said Linda, as if she were divining my thoughts.

"Well, I have been hankering after a second horse," I said slowly.

"Well, we all dream of a second horse, then being horse-mad, we decide we absolutely have to have a third," she said smiling. "One is never enough. But have you considered a very experienced jumper who has been competing for years? That would give you confidence and experience, so you can continue bringing Balius on slowly and not rush him."

"You're an angel of wisdom!" I said, smiling. "And an older horse would not be as expensive as a made-jumper who was ready to compete and get to the top." She smiled back at me.

I slowly rode back to the castle, letting Balius stretch out on a long rein. I gazed around at the landscape of the Scottish Highlands in midwinter, monotonic colours beneath a sky scoured white by the gusting wind. The tops of the hills were iced with snow which merged with the grey clouds.

Balius had done brilliantly today, and he had worked hard. I stuffed him full of treats, put a New Zealand rug on him, and led him up to the field where his mother, Bonnie, was turned out. He trotted up the field towards her. His tail held out like a banner, high-stepping, snorting. I believed that he was rather pleased with himself.

I went back to the castle and fetched writing paper and wrote to the lady who needed a secretary to assist with her memoirs. Her name was Bryony Peach, which I thought was a rather fabulous name, and indicated that perhaps she had had a very interesting life. I told her of my grades at school, which were not brilliant but at least not failing; I listed my own pony books which I had written; described the few pony jobs that I had already undertaken with my friend Ann-Marie; and my current shorthand and typing speeds. And I was available immediately, although it would take me at least a week to drive down there. I had my licence now and had practised towing a horse trailer, but I was still a novice and didn't want to drive for huge distances every day. I walked the dogs back down to the village and put the letter in the post box. Now, it was in the hands of Fate. I hurried back to the castle in time for lunch.

"You're unnaturally quiet today, Jill," said Mummy. She had been chattering on about something to do with the sheep.

"I went down for a lesson with Linda this morning, and I took Balius over the cavalletti grid, preparing him to learn to jump. She suggested that I could benefit from an older, trained horse, a schoolmaster."

"Yes, that would be perfect," said Richard wisely. My step-father was very knowledgeable about horses. "I was thinking you could do with a second horse."

I looked at him in astonishment. He never failed to surprise me in the most delightful manner! Sometimes I thought Mummy should have found him years ago, but I guess she was waiting for the perfect man and in the end, she found him.

"How much money do you have left from selling the two ponies?" asked Mummy.

"I spent a lot on new riding clothes, and some of it has gone on riding lessons with Linda and also paying her to train Balius," I said slowly. "I think I've got about £160 left."

"Well, that's not enough for a new horse, not the sort you want," said Richard.

"How much would this 'schoolmaster' cost?" asked Mummy.

"Well, it would be a horse past its prime, no longer ready to gallop around a three-day event course and try to win, you know, with the steeplechase and the two lots of roads and tracks, as well as the cross-country they have to cover about seventeen miles in all on that second day. But perhaps one that could still do well at one-day events."

"Yes, a one-day event with just the cross-country would be fine, and once you've got enough experience, Balius will probably be ready to step up," said Richard.

"I'm not sure I want to be an eventer," I said, carefully not saying that my experience of Mark Lansdowne had almost put me off eventing for life. "I rather think being a showjumper might suit me better. I've had a lot of experience in the children's classes." Pat Smythe was one of my idols, and I read and re-read her pony books about the Three Jays. I felt a spiritual connection with her.

"Yes, so I guess a horse fifteen-, sixteen- or even seventeen-years-old. And preferably, one schooled to a certain level at dressage would be perfect," I replied thoughtfully.

"Then you could enter the open jumping, Grade C, and also go in some dressage competitions and combined training events," said Richard.

"A promising top-class horse with good basic training could be anything from £1500 and upwards," I said. I had been checking out the advertisements in *Horse and Hound* for some time now.

"I think something in the range of £500 to £1,000 would be quite realistic," said Richard. "I tell you what, your mother and I could contribute half of the cost, but you need to raise the rest yourself."

"Let's hope you get that job," said Mummy, smiling radiantly at me, then at Richard.

I went upstairs to think about this. I was leafing through my back copies of *Horse and Hound,* looking for a schoolmaster. There were a few advertised, but most of them didn't have a price. I hated it when people advertised their horses with no price. I had to hope I got this job with Bryony Peach, but even then, I didn't know what sort of wage she would be offering. When Ann-Marie and I had been working breaking in New Forest ponies, we had been offered £4 a week each. I hoped someone with secretarial skills could ask for more, even if it was a live-in position.

I began to dream of my perfect schoolmaster, a gelding who had once performed well in working hunter classes and trained to advanced level in dressage. I thought I might like a chestnut, I'd never owned a chestnut, but they did say that they were bad-tempered, although I thought that was probably just an old wives' tale.

Chapter Two – Travelling to Cornwall

A week before, I received a reply from Bryony Peach, and she offered me the job, proposing that I be paid £15 per week. I was thrilled, as I had half-expected to be rejected as too young and inexperienced.

I looked up Richard's driving atlas and found that the journey down to Cornwall was more than 700 miles. That was a long way to drive on my own, towing a horse trailer. I felt nervous and feeble. I hated it when I was like this. I was supposed to be brave, independent and always up for a lark. I didn't want Mummy and Richard to know that I was nervous or they would be offering to come with me. I wanted to prove to myself that I could do this. So, I went to Mummy and told her about the letter and that I would drive myself down.

"I'm not sure if that is such a good idea," said Mummy hesitantly. It's a long way; if something goes wrong, you must deal with it yourself. Perhaps John could go with you and then catch the train back. I'm sure Richard wouldn't mind."

"No, Mummy, I don't want that," I said firmly, "I'm determined to do this by myself. I'm almost grown up now."

It was tempting to have John come with me. He was a dependable young man who worked in the stables and would know what to do if something went wrong. But the point was that I should be able to go out there and earn my own living and taking along Richard's staff to help me defeated the object.

I began to look through my clothes. I had all these wonderful new smart clothes and my recently-purchased riding outfits. I also packed some of my comfortable old favourites. I began to day-dream. Perhaps down in Cornwall, I would find a second horse. I didn't want to go to a horse sale and buy something unknown. This purchase was to be proven and tried with a legitimate provenance. I put my Post Office savings book in my suitcase, just in case. I dug through my underwear drawer and found that I had £5 in a card from one of the old aunts, which would also be useful. I had forgotten all about it. One good thing about living here was that decent shops were miles away, so I wasn't tempted to fritter my savings.

Mummy must have been talking to Richard, and by the time we all went down for dinner, he had come up with a rather good plan, a compromise. Yes, I was to drive myself, but he had organised for me to stop along the way and stay with various of his friends who all had stables. And most amazing of all, he had arranged that I spend three days at the David Staley showjumping school in Dorset. I was to join a class for novices that he was running.

"But Balius and I are nowhere near that level yet," I exclaimed.

"No, I explained to him about that, and he has a group called the nursery class, all young horses. You'll probably be top of the class," Richard assured me. He had compiled an itinerary for me:

Night 1 – Thornhill, Flossie and Roman Marlowe

Night 2 – Preston, Ned Sperrit

Nights 3 – Cheltenham, Charles and Venetia Delphinton

Night 4, 5, 6, 7 – Yeovil, David Staley

Night 8 – Dartmoor, the Merrivale Family

Night 9 – Cornwall

"Thornhill isn't there a big castle there, Drumlanrig, I think it is called. Is that where your friends live?" Mummy asked.

"You're thinking that we have a society of castle owners, meeting at a round table wearing tabards," he said with a glint in his eye. "No, I have been to the castle as a visitor, but my friends live in a house that is part of the Buccleuch estate but is rather modest. They have a couple of hunters, a spare stable, and a field for turnout. They would be very happy to put Jill up for a night."

Preston was next on the list, which was very close to Blackpool. I had never been to Blackpool, the Pleasure Beach and the lights.

"So, will there be illuminations?" I asked.

"Well, the lights run in autumn, so you're too late. This is a friend from way back, Ned Sperrit. He is one of the old-school horsemen, where the father passes on his knowledge to his son for many generations. He has all sorts of pills and potions for every occasion. He's been a horse dealer for years, so he might be able to look out a good horse for you. You should talk to him about it."

"He sounds rather unreliable," I said as tactfully as possible, thinking that most horse dealers were horrible swindlers, filing down horses' teeth and up to all sorts of tricks.

"He wouldn't sell you a lemon, don't worry, we go way back," said Richard laughing. "He lives with his sister, who keeps house for him, and they have stables, don't worry, you won't have to padlock the stable door!"

"Cheltenham, something happens in Cheltenham. I just can't quite remember what it is?" I said.

"It is the home of the Cheltenham Gold Cup, the most famous steeplechase after the Grand National. My friends there run a racing stable. They're a very glamorous couple. He was a successful jockey turned trainer, and she is a former fashion model, and they're expecting their first baby. So I thought you might find it interesting to visit a racing stable and see how it runs." Richard looked awfully smug as he imparted this information, like a very clever magician pulling a rabbit out of a hat.

"Wow!" I said. It looked like my social horizons were going to be stretched to the limit with this itinerary. Suddenly life had become incredibly exciting. In fact, it looked rather supersonic at the moment. After the hunter trials last September, when all the guests from the grouse shooting season had gone home, life in the castle had seemed a little grim. It was the type of place that needed lots of people to fill the echoing halls. I can't imagine how Richard had managed all those years without Mummy and me. The weather here in the winter didn't help, the days were so short, and it might be easy to fall into a Slough of Despond.

Christmas had been fun, except we had gone to the Lansdowne's for roast turkey dinner with all the trimmings. This meant I had to sit through a meal with the golden son, Richard's nephew, Mark. He had a beautiful girlfriend who looked like a model and spoke as if she had a plum in her mouth or rather a whole tin of plums. Diana Barton-Tompkin was an Honourable from an old family with unimpeachable antecedents. I felt her x-ray gaze upon me. Her eyes were most extraordinary, enormous and ice-blue in colour. I imagined that they reflected her ice-cold heart.

Diana was from a family who had survived the post-war period without significant loss of their fortune. They stood out from the general crowd of aristocrats who now lived in reduced circumstances. She belonged to a select group from the surviving rump of the Old World. Her family had a large estate in Yorkshire and a sizeable and impressive house in Kensington. However, such ease of position did not translate as it might have to a gracious manner that embraced other people from all walks of life. Diana was of a somewhat malicious turn of character, and she not only knew that her station was rather lofty but made sure that everyone else knew it. According to her class classification, my mother and I were essentially dull middle class.

She was extremely friendly toward Mark and his parents. Even Richard received the benefit of her flashing smile. But she made it obvious in an extremely ungracious way that she looked down her perfect tip-tilted nose at my mother and me as if we were untouchable *parvenus.*

I still hadn't met the Lansdowne's elder son, Horatio, who was to inherit their family estate according to the law of primogeniture. Apparently, he was away bucketing around South America. What if he were to fall in love with me and we should marry, but that would be one in the eye for Malevolent Mark and the Deadly Diana. How they would hate that! This, of course, was an extremely ignoble thought, and had I been more sophisticated, I would have realised that it was a cliché of *"I'll show you!"* Looking back, I think perhaps I could have traded on the notion that we were bohemian, a family of writers who lived simply with high ideals, but Mummy's books were more of the bread and butter sort with no pretensions of art, and my own pony books were part of a genre not recognised at that point in time.

After Christmas dinner, we played charades, and I was abysmally hopeless at it. I had always been rather tunnel-visioned, and despite Mummy's gentle warnings, I would be 'horsey' through and through. Diana was very clever and quick and managed to guess every second item. Her laughter tinkled around the room all evening, and it made me grind my teeth. The Lansdownes were all off to a New Year's Eve party at Diana's parents' place in Yorkshire, which was a Georgian pile, not as large as Blenheim but substantial. We weren't invited.

Instead, Mummy, Richard and I had gone off to the village hall for a local celebration, which was low-key, unpretentious, but extremely jolly. Richard had presented myself and Mummy with his family's tartan, and we wore our new outfits to the party and were reeling all night. It was a rambunctious event, and I began to think that the Scottish people really did know how to celebrate.

I had made a New Year's Resolution that I would dedicate myself totally to Balius's training, but this was hardly a resolution as it had been my intention from the moment I had first seen him. Beyond that, I wasn't exactly sure where I was going. Learning shorthand and German had been a nod towards the notion of further education but living up here in the middle of nowhere. I couldn't quite see where it was going to take me in the long-term. Unless I really did go to a dressage yard in Germany. I wished that I had some crystal ball hovering in mid-air that could show me a clear-cut life but being uprooted from our little town, Chatton, where I had been a big fish in a small equestrian pond, I was floundering around in a sea of uncertain identity.

I began to imagine the scenario of working as a live-in secretary in Cornwall. Bryony Peach would be a wonderful older woman, tall, erect and gracious, who had been a hard woman to hounds all her life, had three husbands, all of whom she has survived, and now wanted to recount her glory days before they faded from her memory. I would sit with a pad and pencil on a stool at her feet and take down her memories, then type them up into a manuscript that would be accepted for publication without a moment's notice.

I was thinking of this woman's life throughout this century when the most astounding news reached me. Or rather, it was astounding that such a thing hadn't happened before. Women were to be allowed to ride in three-day events in the Olympics. Until now, such a sport was considered only suitable for men, even though Sheila Willcox had won a gold medal in the European Championships a few years ago. Now it seemed the old male hierarchy was being forced to reckon with the fact that women could ride just as well as men. This spurred me on, I wanted to prove myself, and I needed a horse ready to compete now, not in a few years. I felt that I was living at the forefront of a new social time, where Diana's world of debutantes was to be rendered obsolete.

Chapter Three – Thornhill and Preston

I made good time on the first leg of my journey south. Cook had prepared a hamper of food for roadside stops and a tin of biscuits for midnight feasts, just in case my various hosts did not give me sufficient for supper. In the early afternoon, I arrived at the small town of Thornhill in the county of Fife. *'The Thane of Fife he had a wife'* kept running through my head like the disordered thoughts of the mad Lady Macbeth. If I remembered correctly, the Thane of Fife's wife and household had been brutally murdered! The main street was very wide and overlooked by an interesting monument. The sky seemed just as wide and big here as it did in the Highlands. Huge, billowing grey and white clouds moved swiftly above our heads, with intermittent patches of blue and sharp yellow sunlight.

Flossie and Roman Marlowe lived on the outskirts of the town. It was not a huge house but looked very comfortable. I wasn't sure what I should call them and decided that Mr and Mrs Marlowe would be respectful unless they asked me to call them Flossie and Roman – I loved that name Flossie and thought that perhaps I would call my daughter that. It was only just after lunch as I had made good time. Mrs Marlowe came bustling out to meet me, wiping her large reddened hands on her apron.

"Mr Marlowe won't be home til later. He's at work. I think we should let that big horse out in the field now, let him stretch his legs after his journey," she said. "Then you must come in and have a nice cup of tea and something to eat."

This sounded good to me. It looked like Mrs Marlowe enjoyed several very good meals every day. She was rather ginormous!

I lowered the ramp, and Balius backed out quietly and obediently. He took no exception to his surroundings and looked around intelligently. He walked off into the field in a dignified manner and dropped his head to try this different flavour of green grass.

Mrs Marlowe took me inside, and we sat down in the kitchen and spent a very comfortable afternoon together. First, we had a gossip, and she wanted to know all about Richard and my mother, the wedding and how things were at the castle. Then we walked along the main street into the town, and while she went to buy food for tea, I went into a very inviting little antique shop. I loved old things and spent quite a lot of time looking at the coloured-glassware and figurines of dogs and horses. I was tempted to buy myself a gorgeous little Welsh pony foal that was a beautiful golden colour with a flaxen mane and tail. Then I thought of my chestnut schoolmaster and decided to save my money.

Mrs Marlowe came by, collected me, and returned to the house. I went out to catch Balius and put him in the stable. He whinnied to the two hunters in the other boxes, and they looked at him with mild curiosity. I went inside and sat at the kitchen table chatting to Mrs Marlowe until her husband returned from work. He matched his wife perfectly as he was a very large man with a florid complexion and small merry black-raisin eyes.

"Young Jill!" he boomed at me, and I felt a huge temptation to giggle at him. His bristly, bushy eyebrows wriggled up and down like caterpillars.

"She's been telling me all about Richard and her mother. It seems like they are love's young dream."

Mr Marlowe roared with laughter as if this was the best joke he'd ever heard. I wasn't quite sure why this was funny.

"How do you know Richard?" I asked curiously.

"Well, that's a story!" said Mr Marlowe and laughed out loud again. He seemed to find his own remarks extremely amusing.

"Richard was a wee lad," said Mr Marlowe, "and we lived up near Blainstock, and he used to come down to our place and play with our children. He was like an only child with his two sisters so much older than him."

After a very large dinner, I offered to help with the washing up, but they wouldn't hear of it. So I went upstairs to bed and sitting up with my pad and pencil and my shorthand book, I virtuously practised some outlines. The following day, I rose early and went out to the stables. I let Balius out in the field so that he could have some open-air time and free exercise, and I went back to muck out his loose box. Mr Marlowe came out and was seeing to the hunters.

"You're a good girl," he boomed at me. "I'm glad Richard has got your mother and you." I smiled politely. I didn't know what to say.

After a huge cooked breakfast of sausages, black pudding and baked beans, I got ready to go, repacking my bag and then going out to load Balius. I was particularly looking forward to my next stop: Ned Sperrit, who might be able to find me the perfect second horse. I had never really met a horse dealer, and I was intensely curious to see such an exotic person in their natural habitat. Unfortunately, Mummy and Ann-Marie's mother had always intimated that 'horse-dealing was not 'the done thing', and when we had asked for more clarity, they had demurred.

I imagined he would be a wizened older man with a flat cap and a northern accent. He would live in a small cottage with a yard out the back with outhouses converted into stables, with a motley collection of different types of horses from children's ponies to 17 hh raking ex-steeplechasers.

Richard had drawn me a map of how to get there, and I found myself in a maze of suburban streets with terraced houses. Finally, I drew up outside an end-of-terrace red-brick house with a large window looking out into the street. I couldn't see a driveway, so I parked on the road, which would not be convenient for other motorists. I walked up to the front door. It was painted green with a big horse-shoe knocker.

No-one answered, and I waited. Then I decided to try around the back and walked down the side of the house.

I shouted out, "Hello! Is there anyone home?"

A dog inside began to yap. I was feeling nervous. I didn't know what I would do if there were no-one here. I couldn't stay parked in the road for long, and I could hear Balius moving around in the trailer. I went back to the front door and banged on the knocker again. Still, no-one appeared. The idea of finding my way out of the labyrinthine streets and back on the road in the dark was a daunting one. I had no idea how one found board and lodging for a horse for the night. Then I heard some shuffling footsteps, and I almost cried out in relief.

"Yes, what d'yer want?" asked a female voice as an old crone opened the door a slit and peered out suspiciously at me.

"I'm looking for Ned Sperrit," I said, wondering if I had come to the wrong house.

"Hummph," she said and opened the door a little wider.

"I'm looking for Mr Sperrit," I said, "Richard Micheldever has arranged that I stay with him tonight. My horse is in the trailer." I gestured towards the road.

"He's round the back, wiv them horses," she said.

"Might you be able to tell him that I am here," I said as politely as I could?

"You need to drive round there, go on down the road, then first on the left, then down the lane, and you are in the yard," she said and shut the door firmly in my face.

I dreaded driving down a narrow alley to find that I wouldn't be able to turn around. I found it very difficult to reverse with a trailer. If you wanted to go one way, then you had to steer the opposite way, and I just couldn't get my mind around it. I would be stuck with no-one to help me. I prayed that the directions she had given me were correct. I started up the Land Rover and turned on the headlights. It was possible that there was a stable yard behind the terrace houses. I could explore on my own two feet first, but I didn't want to leave Balius parked in the street. I had to make a decision. Finally, I decided to trust the old lady, and I drove down the very narrow alley, dodging between the rubbish bins, old tyres and broken pallets.

The headlights were shining into the murky twilight ahead. It began to rain, and I couldn't find the windscreen wipers. I drew to a halt in front of a set of large double gates at the end of alley. Getting out, I was filled with trepidation that I was going to be set upon any minute and not only the Land Rover and the trailer would be stolen but my darling horse. The gates were firmly shut. I banged on them, shouting.

"Ned Sperrit! Ned Sperrit!"

Then slowly, one gate opened, and a little crinkled, wrinkled face peered out with flat cap and a pipe clenched between his teeth.

"You must be Jill!" he said. Now I really did cry with relief.

"I'll open up the gates, you drive in, and we'll get that horse into a stable, warm and snug for the night," he said.

"Thank you, God!" I prayed as I climbed back into the Land Rover. The yard was huge, which was totally surprising. There was a line of very neat loose boxes, and half a dozen horse heads hung over watching us.

"I had no idea there would be a stable yard, in this area, with so many houses," I said, gabbling. I was so relieved.

"Aye, lass, that there is," said Ned with a broad northern accent. "Let's unload the big 'orse and put him to bed."

Balius backed out obediently, and Ned led him over to a loose box on the end of the row. There was a thick clean bed of straw and a hay net hanging from the wall.

"You can park the Land Rover over on that side," said Ned, gesturing. "When you leave in the morning, you can do a full turn. Come on. He'll be right now. Let's go inside and have a cuppa."

He led me beside a muck heap and a pile of old tyres and bits of wood, then we slipped through a broken back fence and walked through a yard full of mud and weeds. We entered the house through the back door.

"Em, it's us," he called, and we sat down at a kitchen table that was piled high with magazines. There were *Horse and Hound*, *The Racing Post*, and *The Field*. What a splendid collection of reading, this could have kept me busy for months!

"Did you used to work with racehorses?" I asked, looking around in a sort of a daze. The kitchen door opened into the drawing-room and it was piled high with little tables, lamps, ornaments that might have been won at a fair. From this section of the house emanated an extremely musty smell. I guessed that Em wasn't the most fastidious of housekeepers!

"Aye, lass, I did, and I was always at the track, now I'm pretty busy with my yard."

"Richard said that you were a dealer?"

"That I am. And I do pretty well with it. They say I've got a good eye for a horse."

"Well, that's interesting because I'm looking to buy a second horse."

"Another like that big grey," said Ned, smiling.

"No, he's only four, five next spring. I'm training him from the beginning. What I would like is something at least 16 hh, aged, a schoolmaster, trained at show jumping and dressage. A horse that I can gain experience on in the adult classes."

"You say he, would you consider a mare?"

"I prefer geldings, but I guess if she were the right mare then yes, I would consider a mare. Oh yes, I was thinking chestnut."

At this, Ned guffawed.

"You ladies, you want your own choice of colour, like it's a frock. You know a good horse is never a bad colour."

"I don't suppose you've got anything like that?" I asked without hope.

"You never know, I have to do a bit of investigating. You know sometimes these good old horses fall upon rough times, they need to be rescued. I suppose if it was in bad condition, you wouldn't mind bringing it back?"

"No, of course not, as long as it wasn't chronically ill or lame, you know so it would never be able to compete again. How much do you think? For what I'm after?" I asked anxiously.

"Richard was good to me many years ago, so I'd give you my best price," said Ned smiling.

Although he was a horse dealer, and he lived in less than pristine conditions, I felt like I could rely on him, which was odd, but I think it is important to follow your intuition sometimes. Besides, Richard wouldn't have arranged for me to stay here unless he could be trusted.

"So, you're off to Cornwall," he said, changing the subject slyly, without telling me a price.

"Yes, I'm to help write the memoirs of a woman called Bryony Peach."

"Well, there's a name from the past," said Ned, his little crinkling eyes getting a faraway look.

"What do you know about her?" I asked. Again, he was evasive.

"You'll soon get to know her if you're writin' her memoirs," he said nodding wisely.

"Now there's Em. She's been down the chippie, you must be 'ungry."

He was right I was starving and the savoury odour of hot fish and chips wafted in through the doorway. I never got an answer to how much for the schoolmaster that I wanted, nor to the ancient history of the life of Bryony Peach. Ned Sperrit was a wily old man, but I liked him tremendously. I would have loved to have read his memoirs, but I didn't imagine he would be forthcoming!

I woke in the morning and had a cup of tea with no milk. Housekeeping was not high on the agenda. I hurried out through the broken back fence, and Balius neighed at me. This absolutely delighted me. He recognised me! The horses' stables were perfect, deep beds of clean straw. That was what was important, cleanliness with the horses, rather than the living conditions of the humans.

As I left, determined to raid Cook's hamper as soon as I was out on the open road and could find a layby, Ned said to me.

"Now lassie, I'll contact Richard when I've found that horse for you."

"That would be absolutely terrific!" I said, against all reason I had every faith in him, I saw the Hand of Providence in this meeting.

Chapter Four – Training Race Horses

That afternoon I arrived at the Delphinton's racing stable. I turned up a long winding driveway edged with elm trees. It seemed to twist back and forth, and then around the corner was the house laid out before me. At first, I thought it was a mirage. It shimmered in the afternoon light, domes and arches of beautiful pale pink shiny stone, the house seemed to be floating on a green velvet sward that sat upon a blue-as-blue lake with a mirror-like surface upon which floated a pair of swans. Later I was told by Venetia that the house was Palladian, made of pink marble.

This was as different to Ned Sperrit's house, as chalk from cheese. Hopping from one exotic place to another, was like peeking through the keyhole at all different types of lifestyles. I drove on around the back, following a rather fancy sign in scrolling letters that said 'To The Stables'.

The brick-built stable yard was not as ornate and elaborate as the house, but there was a fancy statue of a full-size beautiful galloping horse in full flight in the centre of the yard; a clock tower; and wooden boxes overflowing with pale yellow spring flowers. This was certainly the most stylish stable yard I had ever set eyes on.

I pulled up in the parking area, and a groom rushed over to greet me and tell me I was expected. They had rung through to the house to tell them I had arrived and Mrs Delphinton would be here in a minute. I felt as if I were royalty!

"Oh! Jill darling!" gushed a woman who glided towards me, on a pair of sparkling high heels. I began to wonder if I hadn't blundered onto a film set. She was an utterly divine sight, a fitting chatelaine for the magical house.

"Richard rang this morning to remind me that you were expected. We've been so looking forward to meeting you. Dear Richard - said you were a wonderful young woman."

I stood there feeling a little less than wonderful, my mouth open. Compared to this vision in high heels and a floating gauzy silver garment, I was in scruff order. Thank goodness I had packed my smart new clothes. I felt an immediate need to get inside, have a bath, wash my hair and put on at least my second-best dress, which was respectable but would look rather dowdy next to Venetia's splendiferous and out of this world sartorial creations.

Balius was his usual intelligent self, but he wasn't overcome with the elegance of his surroundings. He was such a gentleman, he could take it in his stride. I only wished that I had a modicum of his nonchalance.

"Come on, darling," said Venetia. Her hand was very small and elegant, and I could only wonder at the huge bumpy rings that adorned her tiny white fingers, undoubtedly, they would be priceless gems. I found myself being towed into the marble palace as if I were being dragged into someone else's dream of paradise.

We entered through the grandest back door I had ever seen. It was shaped like an arch and above it was moldings of cherubs. I got pulled along enthusiastically by the evanescent Venetia. There was an air of unreality about all this, like a mirage hovering above a foaming wave that would slip back into the sea. Then I determined that I should enjoy it. Venetia had this wonderful gift of making one feel special, and I allowed her fairy dust to rub off on me.

When we were seated in Venetia's boudoir, she tinkled a small silver bell and told the neat Mediterranean-looking servant to bring us tea with chocolate biscuits, giggling conspiratorially as if we were small children raiding the pantry.

The tea was not to my taste, Lapsang Souchang, very sweet and flowery. I much preferred builder's tea, in which my spoon could stand up. I decided that I was far too plebian for this rarified atmosphere. Still, it was fascinating, even if I did feel like a baby elephant lumbering through a porcelain display. As well as the most delicious chocolate biscuits I had ever tasted there were tiny fairy cakes loaded with pink and white icing, and crunchy silver baubles, mouthfuls of pure heaven.

Venetia chattered on about her husband, Charles. Apparently, he was away at the races with three of the horses. He was a horse race trainer, specialising in steeplechasers and that is why they lived so close to Cheltenham. This I found fascinating. Mummy would never take me to the races, saying it wasn't suitable, a bit like 'horse dealers'. She would never elaborate as to exactly why it was not suitable. I'm not sure what she would have made of this setup. Suddenly I felt so commonplace, my world of riding lessons and gymkhanas was not in this league!

After tea, Venetia told me she had to lie down and rest as she was pregnant with a baby called Archibald. I had not even noticed the baby bump, she carried it so lightly. The servant would show me to my room. At seven, there were drinks in the drawing-room before dinner. She suggested that I might like to wander around the house, the library was very interesting, apologising profusely, but she was just too weary to take me herself.

I was rather relieved to be left to my own devices in this most extraordinary place. I was thrilled at the invitation to explore, but first I needed a bath and to get changed into my second-best dress. I also wanted to go back out to

the stables and ask the staff if Balius could be put out in a field for a few hours. After travelling in the trailer, I felt that he would appreciate a bit of fresh air and freedom.

After I had bathed and changed, I made my way back to the stables and spoke to the man who appeared to be the Stable Manager. He gestured to the loveliest field, positively Arcadian in aspect, with large trees overhanging a field shelter and sweet green untrampled grass. Balius looked around approvingly and walked off snatching a mouthful here and there.

I went back into the house and wandered through corridors, peeking into superlatively grand rooms, with high ceilings, brocade-clad walls and intricately-decorated cornices. I particularly loved the paintings, rather than the stern and ugly ancestors that usually decorated the walls of such grand houses. The Delphintons favoured beautiful watercolours – lots of shimmering water, endless delicately-tinted skies, dreamy ships and people drifting across the scenery.

The gong rang for dinner, and I searched around until I found a servant who directed me to the drawing-room where we were to meet for drinks. I walked in, and Venetia tripped over to me in her high heels.

"Jill darling, come and meet my handsome Charles."

I wondered if she ever talked in an ordinary way, this lilting affected manner of speech might be rather tiring to keep up.

Charles was, as was to be expected, an extraordinarily handsome man. He looked like a film star, with a firm square jaw, the bluest of blue eyes, and beautiful blond hair brushed back in wings.

"Good evening Jill," he said, holding his hand out for a firm handshake.

"Good evening," I found myself stumbling over the words.

"Jill is off on a mission; she is to help Bryony Peach write her memoirs."

"Bryony Peach!" exclaimed Charles. "My goodness, that will be exciting!" My ears perked up at this.

"Do you know Miss Peach?" I asked.

"I met her once, years ago, but I know her by reputation. Did you know that she lived in Kenya during World War Two, she was there when Joss Hay was murdered, I think she knew June Carberry."

I racked my brains, but I had no idea who Joss Hay or June Carberry were, or anything at all about a murder. It did sound tremendously exciting. My imagination took off at top speed, and I saw myself feted as the raconteur of

the most interesting and colourful tale of the century, Africa, murder, aristocracy and intrigue. My eloquent writing would bring me fame and a reputation as a writer of the first order.

"Could you tell me a little more about Joss Hay?" I asked politely.

"He was an aristocrat with the reputation of a philanderer who married Lady Idina Gordon, and they went to Kenya. They were part of that notorious Happy Valley set. Before he left England, he was involved with the British Union of Fascists."

"And he was murdered?" I asked my eyes wide with astonishment.

"Yes, he was shot at point-blank range. He was having an affair with a woman called Diana Broughton, and she was leaving her husband, and then Joss was shot. It was a huge thing at the time. Diana's husband was tried for his murder but found not guilty."

"Goodness, but how was Bryony Peach involved?" I asked.

"I don't really know, but there were a lot of wild rumours flying around."

"I had no idea," I gasped. The enormity of what he was telling me began to sink in. Venetia began chattering on to her husband, and I was left to think.

We trooped along the corridor to a long dining-room, and the meal was served in the most beautiful dinner service that I had ever seen, green and gold patterned plates and bowls, with silver flatware covering the polished wooden table.

"We are looking forward to meeting your mother, Richard tells us that she is an absolute treasure."

It was hard to think of an answer to this remark.

"And apparently young Mark's nose is rather out of joint," said Venetia laughing softly.

"Have you met Horatio yet?" asked Charles.

"No, apparently he's in South America."

"Horatio is an absolute darling, we adore him," said Venetia.

My ears pricked up at that. I quite often indulged in the fantasy that Horatio should fall in love with me, and we would form an alliance that would well and truly put Malevolent Mark in his place.

"What is Horatio like?" I asked innocently.

"He's great fun, doesn't take himself at all seriously. He can ride too, as a boy he was a much better rider than Mark. He's a very adventurous type of person and is apparently enjoying his travels."

"He sounds great fun," I replied.

"Which Mark is not!" said Venetia. Charles frowned at her as if warning her not to be indiscreet. But I got the impression that Venetia, despite her fragile appearance, did whatever she wanted as the mood took her. I was curious to know more but thought that I should have talked to Venetia about this earlier, without Charles being around. She was so delightfully frank and chatty that she might have given me more information about the inside story of the Lansdowne family.

Charles changed the subject by turning to me and asking if I would like to ride Balius out with the first-string tomorrow morning, onto the gallops for training. I was utterly thrilled.

"I would love that!" I said.

"We can lend you an exercise saddle, and you can have a go at riding very short."

I had often wondered how it must feel to be on top of a huge galloping horse, and now it seemed that I was going to find out. I hoped that I wasn't going to fall off. I imagined Balius getting so excited, and he would bolt and perched precariously above him I wouldn't have a hope of sticking on. But I had to have a go, as long as I didn't fall off, I was sure that it would feel out of this world.

One of the servants came to my bedroom very early with a mug of tea. This time it was PG Tips, not that horrible flowery Lapsang thing. It was still pitch-black outside, and I got dressed in my best riding clothes, if I was going to be carted off to hospital, then I wanted to look professional. I gave myself a talking to about negativity, if one creates a reality through one's imagination then I must envisage Balius galloping with the best of them, and me riding as if I were in the Grand National, like Velvet Brown.

I managed to gulp down the tea with two sugars to give me energy and courage. Then I hurried down to the stables. I wanted to be the one to saddle up Balius and then I could mount before we went out and work out how to ride in such a tiny saddle. I wondered whether I should push my boot right through the stirrup in jockey-style or stick to my usual ball of the foot on the stirrup bar, in case I fell off, I didn't want to get dragged. This was the nightmare scenario that I was trying to banish from my mind.

Balius picked up on my nervousness, and his ears were swivelling around, listening to the bustle in the stable yard. He sidestepped as I put the saddle

on his back. It was tiny, and I was filled with trepidation. I had no idea how I was going to mount. The yard was very busy, with stable lads, and the odd lass leading out the first string. We went up in groups of eight. I led Balius out and wondered whether I should have asked to borrow a running martingale. Although I generally disapproved of the use of martingales, when the correct head position of the horse should be achieved by good riding, I couldn't quite see how one should use one's legs when they were bent above the saddle.

The Assistant Trainer came over and motioned to me that he was going to give me a leg up. I felt myself thrown in the air, and I landed with a bit of a thump. Balius flinched beneath me, and I held him steady with my legs wrapped around his sides. Then I thrust my feet into the very light stirrups. It felt totally weird, but if all the others could do it, then I didn't see why I couldn't. They were riding around in a circle, and Charles was there in his waxed cotton jacket and flat tweed cap, shouting out instructions, critically appraising each horse, looking for unevenness of stride. When everyone was mounted, and each horse checked, we made our way out of the gate in single file and rode down beside the road. The gallops were on the racecourse and we entered by a small gate at the bottom end of the course.

Can you imagine how exciting it is to gallop around a racecourse? Of course, women could not be jockeys at this point, but who knows in the future what might be possible? Balius was tittupping around, but I spoke to him quietly and kept him one horse's length behind the horse in front. I tried to keep him tucked in so that he would settle in his place. He was much thicker set and tubbier than the other horses, who were lightly built and all muscle and sinew.

Charles gave instructions to trot around the course once then a half gallop from a certain marker. Rising at the trot with your stirrups almost in your armpits was not easy, I can assure you, but after a while, I got the hang of it. However, I continued to feel extremely insecure. We trotted all the way around, and Balius became more and more excited and began to pull and canter sideways trying to race. There were a bunch of other horses galloping on the far side and sweeping around towards us. I imagined Balius was going to leap out of his skin and take off and I would be perched like a monkey on his neck before I took a crashing fall.

We completed the first circuit, and the other horses in the line took off at a thundering pace, it was meant to be a half-gallop, but I felt like I had never been so fast in my life. I sat forward, and my hands moved back and forth with the motion of Balius's head. Then I forgot my fears and fell into the thrall of the excitement of speed, wind and air rushing past me. I even

wondered whether we could pull out and overtake those in front, but Balius was beginning to fall back, he just didn't have the speed or the fitness, he was outclassed. This was hardly surprising!

I think I was as unfit as Balius, my face bright red and finding it hard to get my breath. This had been such an interesting experience. All too soon we rode in single file at the walk back to the stables. I put Balius in his loose box and rubbed him down. I could still feel the adrenaline coursing through my body. The second string was mounted and going out, and I watched them wishing that I could have another go, this time on one of the racehorses. When they returned, we all trooped inside to the large kitchen and sat around a huge table for breakfast. The camaraderie, banter and joking were great fun, not to mention the mountains of crisp bacon, perfectly fried eggs and toast and chunky marmalade.

Then the staff drifted back to their quarters, and I bid Venetia and Charles farewell and set off on the next leg of my journey. I was bound for David Staley's yard for the showjumping clinic.

Chapter Five – Show Jumping Horror!

I arrived at the yard of David Staley and vaguely remembered what people had said about him, that he was a maverick. I wasn't sure exactly what that meant, and I was a little nervous. Balius had behaved so well yesterday racing around with the steeplechasers but perhaps he wasn't ready for a gruelling three-day showjumping clinic.

Mr Staley didn't make an appearance when I arrived; and a very thin, loutish-looking youth showed me Balius's stable. It was cleanish, but not pristine. There were other horse heads looking over the half-doors, and Balius looked around with his bold, intelligent gaze, his small neat ears swivelling.

I settled him in and brought him a feed from my supply in the trailer and refilled his hay net and gave him his own bucket filled with water from the tap in the yard. The thin lad had disappeared, and there was no-one around. I wasn't sure what I should do. In the end, I parked the Land Rover and trailer around the corner and walked tentatively up to the back door of the rambling old house beside the stable yard. I knocked on the door, but there was no response.

I stood there, shifting my weight from one leg to another. It was late afternoon, and the clouds had massed on the horizon, threatening a storm. I wondered if the clinic would be on the following day, there didn't look to be an indoor riding school anywhere. I knocked again, this time very loudly.

"Alright, alright!" said a woman who opened the door. She had greasy lanky hair hanging over her forehead and a dirty apron and slippers. "There's no need to make such a racket."

"I've come for the three-day clinic with David Staley, the erh.." I stumbled in the face of her hostile look. I was even wondering if I had come to the right place, perhaps I had blundered into quite another establishment. I was about to turn tail and take Balius and keep driving.

"Alright, alright," she muttered, "you're early, there's no-one else here yet, I suppose you better come in."

This was hardly the warmest welcome. Inside the house was worse than the outside, ingrained dirt on the walls, dust lay thick on the skirting boards, and it smelt of wet dog. It's not that I am a house cleaner of the highest order, but there is a certain standard that one should try and attain. I imagined the face that Mummy would pull if she was here with me now. I had come to

realise what an eclectic bunch of friends Richard had, but I was seriously wondering about this one, he seemed a bit of a dud.

Finally, a few more riders wandered in and then over supper, we met the man himself. He looked like a ferret, not that I had anything in particular against ferrets. He had narrow eyes that darted this way and that, underneath thick bristly eyebrows, decidedly shifty! I was shown up to a bedroom which I was to share with one of the other girls. The beds were old and saggy with springs that must have seen better days.

The other girl was from Hampshire, constantly referring to 'my people' in a very exaggerated posh accent. I asked her about her horse and she said her father had bought him off Lord Didsbury and this seemed to be his defining feature. I was a little tempted to talk about Blainstock Castle but decided that I would maintain a lofty silence. Otherwise, I would be a tawdry social climber, as bad as her.

The next day we all mucked out the stables of our own horses. Balius was his usual cheerful self, and I was glad that our sordid surroundings had had no ill-effect upon him. We straggled out to the arena and rain was threatening from a black sky. We walked in a dispirited circle. There was a couple of jumps in the centre of the ring. They were flimsy with no wings and no ground lines, to give the horses something with which to assess the height accurately. I became increasingly depressed.

David Staley came out striding around, slapping his whip against his long boots in an arrogant fashion. We were only three, and we walked in desultory fashion around in a circle.

"Come on kids, liven up the nags, jiggle the bits, kick them a little, get them up to the mark."

I looked at him in horror – KICKING – was the worst sin of all time as far as I knew.

I nudged Balius a little with my heels. He shook his head as if to say, 'what's the matter with you!'

"Now I want you to canter a couple of circles and then over the jump in the middle. It was only two feet high but was an exceedingly uninviting obstacle. So far, I had been ultra-careful with Balius, jumping over a few small natural obstacles always with a lead from an experienced horse, and the cavallettis at Linda's. This was awful, not at all what I was expecting.

The girl I had shared a room with was to go first. Her mount purchased from Lord Didsbury was a big blood horse, with a fiery temperament. She had him pulled in on a short rein and needled him with her heels. Then a very tall boy with lanky brown hair went next on a sluggish fat pony.

"Give him a taste of the whip," said David. "You need to liven him up!"

This was getting worse by the minute. I quietly gave Balius the aids to canter on. He was going so well, light on the bit, lots of impulsion and a bouncy regular stride, I felt so proud of him.

"You two!" said David. "Get him moving!" I nearly spat back at him with a reply that he was moving and jolly well, but I shut my mouth in a thin, determined line. We continued to canter around. Then the girl on the blood horse headed towards the jump. Her horse was going sideways, and it was all she could do to keep a hold on him. He jumped wildly and hit the pole with his front legs.

"That's not good," said David. Talk about stating the obvious! "He needs to learn a lesson." This sounded ominous. The tall boy approached the jump next, and his lazy pony refused. He wheeled around and went at it flourishing his whip and whacking the pony's flanks. But again, the fat pony ground to a halt.

"Let the big grey through," shouted David.

With some trepidation, I cantered towards the jump, I felt Balius baulk a little, as in 'what on earth is this?' but I closed my legs and murmured encouragement to him, and he bounced over.

"That was brilliant," I said softly stroking his neck as we cantered on around the circle.

"Well done the grey," said David, obviously not remembering my name. "Now I'm going to get behind Fatso with the whip," he shouted flourishing a lunge whip and flicking it across the backs of the unfortunate pony's hind legs above the hocks. This time the fat pony did manage to heave himself over the jump, like a tired, dispirited elephant.

"Now, let's sort out the careless jumper," said David. "You on the grey hold the reins of Fatso and you boy can help me."

He stood on one side of the jump, and the boy stood on the other. The blood pony cantered in sideways again and took another wild leap in the air. He would have cleared the jump, but David and the boy lifted the pole as he went over and gave him a sharp, stinging rap across his front legs.

I gasped, my mouth opening and closing like a fish. Of course, I had heard of rapping, as this process was called but I didn't know anyone who actually did it. Although it was relatively widely practised, I personally couldn't see the logic in it. If the horse were to learn to judge the height of a jump and how much he had to leap to get over, then this seemed deliberately misleading.

"It would probably do them all good to be rapped," said David.

It was at this point that I lost my good manners.

"I've got a headache," I lied, "I'm going back inside. I can't ride for another minute."

I could have told him exactly why I didn't approve, but I didn't have the words or the authority to carry it off. I was determined to get out of there as soon as possible. If I had to sleep in the Land Rover on the side of the road, we were leaving! I dismounted, handed the reins of the fat pony to the boy and walked away.

I put Balius in his stable, made sure he had hay and water and went inside. I went up to my room to think. I really didn't want to stay here another minute. It was absolutely awful. I knew that Richard had meant well and had paid for me to have three days' training, but this was going to be disastrous. I found my travel itinerary carefully written out by Richard and saw with relief that the next stop, the Merrivales had a phone number. I crept back down the stairs and dialled their number. Just as someone picked up, I heard the back door open. I gave a guilty start, but it was only the drab housekeeper. I turned my back towards her and muttered into my hand, cupped around the speaker of the phone.

"Is that Mrs Merrivale?"

"Yes, it is my love," said a very jolly voice.

"This is Jill. I'm meant to be coming to your place in two days' time, I wondered if I could come sooner, like late tonight," I whispered.

"Yes, certainly, my love. Is there something wrong? You sound a little strained."

"I can't talk about it. I'll be with you shortly."

I rushed up to my bedroom and threw things in my bag and tumbled back down the stairs.

"Family emergency," I gasped to the housekeeper. "I'm so sorry I have to go." I literally ran out of the house round to the Land Rover, started it up and drove into the stable yard. Leaving the engine running, I picked up my tack and threw it in the back and then led Balius out. He was always good to load, and I just hoped that this wouldn't be the day that he refused to co-operate.

I pulled down the tailgate and paused for a moment to take a deep breath. I was being melodramatic even if the Dastardly David returned at this minute, he could hardly stop me from leaving. I wasn't a prisoner here.

Balius was watching me as if he thought I was behaving rather strangely. However, he obediently followed me up the ramp. I tied him up and ducked under the chest bar and down the ramp which I threw up.

Then I jumped into the driving seat and put the Land Rover into first gear, and we were heading down the lane back to the main road. I felt as if I had the demons from hell on my tail. As we drove, I began to calm down and wondered whether I wasn't being a drama queen. Was it really that bad? Rapping? I didn't know, but from the first moment I'd arrived at that place, it just didn't feel right. I would have to ring Mummy and Richard and make some excuse. Now I had to drive to my next stop. It was quite a short leg only about eighty miles. If it was as lovely as it sounded, then perhaps I could stay on for a few days, so I didn't arrive at my new job before the appointed time.

Chapter Six – The Jolly Merrivales

I drove, and I drove, and I tried to see the positive. Balius had jumped that awful jump very well. It wasn't in my plan, but he had managed it without a problem. In fact, he had been a dream ever since we had left. He seemed to enjoy the constant activity, the change in scenery and all the new places we were visiting together. I got to the edge of the Dartmoor National Park and I was calmed by the tranquil empty beauty. Then I saw my first wild ponies, such feisty, hairy little bundles of pony joy.

It took a while to drive along the very narrow roads, and, finally, I got to the Merrivale house late in the afternoon, golden sunshine streaming softly onto the long low white-washed walls with a chimney at each end of a rambling house. I drove past the front door and kept going and arrived in a well-swept and very neat stable yard. Beyond that, I could see the cow barn, and it looked just like a proper farm, a really 'farmy' looking farm. Two young people were scrubbing out buckets next to the tap.

"Hello! Hello!" they shouted, with broad smiles on their freckled faces. "You must be Jill!"

It was such a heart-warming welcome, like a hot foamy bath after my last stop and I climbed out of the Land Rover and felt like bursting into tears. This was a family where I fitted in, properly horsey in the very best tradition. I felt like I was back in a familiar world.

"Hello," I called, dashing the tears out of my eyes with the back of my hand.

"We'll help you unload. We're dying to see this amazing horse that Richard was telling our father about. They pulled down the ramp, and Balius turned his head to look at them.

"Oh yes, he is a beauty," said the boy.

"I say, you're right," said the girl.

I felt so grateful for their enthusiasm and cheerfulness.

"Well, I do rather love him," I admitted. "But tell me your names?"

"I'm Olly, and this is Sandy, she's my sister, well I suppose you worked that out."

"Olly, Sandy," I said thinking there were five children and I was going to have to learn all their names and these two did look very similar, broad smiling freckled faces and frizzy brown hair.

They led Balius into a very spacious loose box with sweet-smelling straw thatched into a deep bed.

"I've brought my own hay," I said. "It's what he's used to."

"Yes, horses do like their routine, don't they, and you should be very careful when you change their feed," said Olly wisely.

Then I knew that these were proper horsey people, the sort of people, like myself, who understood each other immediately.

Once Balius was settled, Sandy took my hand in such a jolly and kind way that I felt like I had found my second family.

"Come inside," she said, "the others are dying to meet you. We love having visitors here."

I followed them in through the back door of the big white house and straight into a very large warm kitchen that was scented with the smell of freshly baked bread. The three other children tumbled into the room, laughing and pushing each other, and they did all look remarkably alike. Shiny polished kitchen implements were hanging over a huge Aga, with a pot of steaming stew simmering.

"Rosie, Posy and Button, our youngest boy, and isn't he as cute as a button." Quite understandably, the youngest little Merrivale squirmed at his mother's description. They were certainly a rambunctious, noisy, fun family. Mrs Merrivale was very jolly and matronly, as comfortable as a big squashy sofa. I wondered what it might have been like if I had had bundles of brothers and sisters in a lively, noisy house, like a Pullein-Thompson family.

"Do you have horses, there were none in the stables?" I asked.

"Our ponies are mainly Dartmoor, at least crossbred, they're hardy so, we let them out in the big field during the day, it makes them much happier," said Rosie.

"That sounds good," I said. "Balius is a quarter Highland, and he goes out a lot, he and his mother Bonnie are turned out together, they seem to love each other still."

"Well, tomorrow we can go for a ride in the morning up on the moors and then he can go out, I gather you've been on the road for days."

"I'm sure he'd love that," I said. "Riding on the moors sounds wonderful."

"Sit down my love and have a nice cup of tea. Then it's time to bring the ponies in for the night. I guess you would like to see them."

"Oh yes rather, how many do you have?"

"There's five of the ponies, and then Mr Merrivale has a big hunter. He needs a big horse as he's a rather large man," said Mrs Merrivale, her deep laughter rumbling out of her.

We walked through the stable yard in a big group, each of the children was swinging a halter, and I was given one for Mr Merrivale's hunter. The ponies and the horse were all waiting at the gate, milling around, trying to be the first to get out.

"They're lovely!" I exclaimed. "Oh, I love that little brown one with the light-coloured nose, as if it has been dipped in a bucket of meal."

"That's Twinkle. She's the smallest. We have all ridden her and then she gets passed on to the next one. But she's a rocket when it comes to riding cross-country, she can keep up with anything."

They were all different shades of brown and bay, with gorgeous thick manes and tails, except Mr Merrivale's hunter who was a bright chestnut cob with very thick legs and a short thick neck.

We led them in a bunch to the stable, and they all dashed to their respective loose boxes looking for their evening feeds. Once they were settled, we trooped into the house, and Mrs Merrivale served up beef stew with huge fluffy dumplings and big helpings of fresh carrots and peas. After we had eaten, they took me up to the first floor, and I had the guest room. It was painted the most cheerful egg-yolk yellow with bright blue curtains, and everything smelled fresh and clean. I had a bath, cleaned my teeth and snuggled down into my extremely comfortable bed. I had planned on practising my shorthand, but my eyelids were heavy, and I just had time to switch the light out, and I was sound asleep.

The next morning was a big cooked breakfast, and I helped wash the dishes and the others rushed to the stable yard to muck out. Mrs Merrivale had packed up some supplies, and we were going to have a morning tea when we got to the top of the tor. Apparently, it was the best view.

Balius was so much bigger than the little ponies but they could move, and they knew the tracks. We had to work hard to keep up with them. We went up and down steep slopes and across the crest of rolling hills and then they showed me the tor in the distance, a huge rock on top of the steepest hill. The weather was warm with white cotton wool clouds and the smell of freedom in the air. I was so glad to be here when I might have been sweating over shorthand, typing and book-keeping in secretarial college.

It took much longer to get to the top of the tor than it had seemed and finally, we dismounted, and the ponies began to crop the green grass that grew around the base of the rocks. We ate buttered currant buns and swigged orange squash out of bottles.

"This is a wonderful place to live," I said.

"But you've got moorland up in the Highlands," said Rosie.

"Yes, but it is starker than this, not the same, somehow empty," I said, not quite sure how it was different - but it was. Perhaps it was being in the throng of such happy company that made the difference.

We got back in time for a late lunch. First, we let Balius and the ponies go in the field. My big grey horse did look a little incongruous next to his much smaller Moorland counterparts, but he seemed very happy. We went into the house, and I had that fantastic feeling of being tired and hungry and full of fresh air.

"What would you like to do this afternoon, Jill?" asked Mrs Merrivale.

"You really don't need to entertain me," I protested, "I am so enjoying staying here. I think I should go upstairs and try and practise my shorthand. I'm worried that my speed is not going to be fast enough."

"I could dictate something to you," said Rosie helpfully, "and we can time you."

Everyone thought this was a great idea, and they outdid themselves dictating silly things to me and then asking me to read it back to them. Sometimes I got it right but other times what I read back to them was even sillier than the original dictation. I did appreciate their help. Then Sandy offered to show me her pony book collection. She was the bookworm of the family and very proud of her collection that included over forty books. Two of her favourites were "Moorland Mousie" and "Older Mousie" by Golden Gorse.

"I just love that name – Golden Gorse," she told me. We sat there looking through the beautiful Lionel Edwards drawings. Then we tried copying the drawings ourselves, but the results were not brilliant. It was gratifying that she actually had one of my pony books in her collection, and I promised to send her copies of the others.

The next day we rode again, this time in the opposite direction to the top of another hill from where we could see the sea in the distance.

"You should all come up to Scotland to visit the castle," I suggested.

"Yes, Mr Micheldever has invited us, but it is rather far, and we don't like to leave the ponies."

We got back to the farm and enjoyed some more delicious and substantial meals. Although I felt like I could stay here forever, I decided that I might outstay my welcome and telephoned Bryony Peach and asked her if I might arrive the next day.

The Merrivales all came out and waved good-bye. They were wonderful people, and I had quite forgotten my bad experience at David Staley's. I drove south and crossed the River Tamar and then I was in Cornwall. It definitely seemed different. It was meant to be a magic land of piskies, Cornish pasties, tin mines and smugglers. It was somehow full of mysterious promise, like in a children's adventure storybook.

I was beginning to get excited. I had never been to Cornwall before, and I began to feel as if something very important and very exciting was going to happen to me. I began to imagine all sorts of scenarios such as galloping across the moors in the dead of night, wearing a long black cape after discovering the secret plans of wicked smugglers, stumbling upon some long-lost treasure and being given a stupendous reward. Then reality thrust itself upon me, and I would probably find that Bryony Peach was absolutely batty and spouting nonsense and my job would last less than week, and I would have to drive all the way back having spent more on petrol than my paltry wage. Of course, I had no idea that I would find myself in league with the smugglers and profiting from their illegal trade, but as usual I am running too far ahead of myself.

The road down through Cornwall lay along the spine of the peninsula, and my destination was very near somewhere called Lamorna Cove, which was apparently an idyllic little cove very popular with holidaymakers, or swivel necks as they called them in Cornwall, due to the fact that they spent their holidays looking at everything around them.

In some places, the Cornish peninsula is only seven miles wide. and if you go to the top of the hill, you can see both the Atlantic Ocean and the English Channel. Lamorna Cove was on the side of the English Channel and not far from the famous Minack Theatre which was an open-air amphitheatre built by a woman called Rowena Cade in Victorian times.

I followed the map and arrived in a very cosy green valley, protected from the sea gales that sometimes swept across the landscape. The road was so narrow that I wondered if we would make it without scraping the high stone walls on either side. It would be impossible if we met an oncoming car, and there was no way I would be able to reverse.

Chapter Seven – Working in Hidden Valley

I was feeling increasingly nervous as I approached Bryony Peach's house. She had sent me some very detailed instructions and a rough map so I knew that I should be able to find it, but I was more and more concerned that I just wasn't going to be up to the job. I doubted that my shorthand was sufficiently fast, or even worse, I would take it all down and then not be able to interpret my own squiggles. I hoped that she wasn't going to be a dragon, all governessy and mean, worse than the teachers at school. On the other hand, she might be entirely insane and be spouting gibberish, and somehow, I would either have to make sense of it or make some excuse to leave.

I had had such a wonderful time at the Merrivales that I began to wish that perhaps they would adopt me. I would make rather a good big sister to that large family and having so many brothers and sisters would be awfully jolly. We could spend all day riding around the moor, schooling the ponies and making plans for the summer. Now it looked like I was going to be stuck in a valley away from ordinary human beings, the constant companion of an old lady.

The driveway to the house was overhung with tree branches, and I could hear them scraping on the roof of the trailer. Balius was moving uneasily.

"Hang in there boy, we're nearly there," I shouted out the window.

The house looked as if it were sinking into the ground like it had been there a long time. It was long and low with overhanging eaves. The walls were coated with green lichen. There was a sense of ancient decay, no sign of life. I hoped that the accommodation for Balius was going to be satisfactory. No falling down fences through which he could escape.

I pulled up in the driveway and made my way to the front door, peeling blue paint and worn wood. I knocked tentatively. A little dog was yapping. I knocked again, and the dog continued to bark. I began to have serious doubts. Perhaps Bryony Peach was so old and decrepit that she really needed a carer, not a secretary. I gave myself a mental shake; anyone can take their time to answer the door; it didn't mean they were approaching dementia.

I knocked for the third time, and then I heard footsteps. A tall, gaunt woman answered the door, wiping her hands on a tea towel.

"I was in the middle of the washing," she said.

I sighed with relief; she was obviously still sound in wind and limb.

"Good afternoon Mrs Peach," I hazarded a guess that she might have been married. Hadn't someone told me she had been married three times? Or was that merely my imaginings?

She smiled at me; a rather prim, tight smile, her lips stretched over teeth glinting with gold fillings.

"You must be Jill," she said, "I've been waiting for you to arrive. Now we can get to work and put these memoirs to bed before I fall off the perch."

I felt that this allusion to her own death was a little startling. It was hard to guess how old she might be, she was certainly old, her skin hanging in folds, but her stance was upright, and she was thin.

"Let's sort out the horse first then you must come in, and we can talk about the memoirs."

She stood back while I let the ramp down. I slipped in and untied Balius, and he backed out quietly and carefully.

"He is a nice lump of a horse," said Bryony approvingly. "Follow me."

We walked on a cracked concrete path around the corner of the house, and there was a long and narrow field with a three-sided stone paddock shelter, with its back to the wind.

"We've got no stables, but he'll be snug in the shelter when the weather is bad. Most horses would rather be out than in stables anyway. We can order hay from the local farmer, and there's a produce store down in Penzance for his corn."

"What is the riding around here like?" I asked. Hoping that I didn't sound like I'd come for a riding holiday rather than a job of work.

"There's lots of bridle paths, and the roads are fairly quiet in winter, and then you can get up on to the moor. Is he good in traffic?"

"He's not too bad, although there isn't much traffic up in the Highlands in Scotland."

"You can ride down to the beach. There's the cove but not long stretches of sand here. You could ride him round to Marazion and gallop him across the sands there."

"Sounds great," I said.

I led him through the gate and noticed that it was sturdy, and the stone fences looked quite high and in good repair. The walls of the valley also made a natural barrier.

"He'll be fine," said Bryony. "I was thinking I might borrow the old pony from Mr Bell down the road, that way he'll have company."

"That would be fantastic," I said. "Horses are herd animals, and he could get quite lonely."

A hot rush of embarrassment swept over me, and my face was like a beaming red tomato. This last sentence sounded so preachy, any horse person worth their salt knew that horses were herd animals. I must sound like I was teaching my grandmother to suck eggs.

I hurried back to the horse trailer to hide my confusion and fetched Balius's hay net and hung it on a hook high on the wall of the paddock shelter. I checked the trough which had been scrubbed out recently and filled with a hosepipe which ran from a tap at the back of the house.

"You've prepared it for him!" I exclaimed.

"I've had a lot of horses throughout my life," said Bryony, "it's good to have another one in the field after all these years." I thought she sounded a little wistful as she said this. We went back around to the Land Rover, and I fetched my bag, which was filled with clothes that needed washing. She ushered me inside. The ceiling was very low, and I had to duck my head as I came through the doorway.

"Down the corridor and third on the left is the guest bedroom."

It was a very spacious room with two bay windows that looked over the front lawn, which was more moss than grass. There was even a glimpse of the sea in the distance through the bare branches of the trees. The walls looked like they needed re-painting, but it had obviously been aired recently and swept and dusted.

"I had my char come in and give it a good bottoming," she told me.

"It is very pleasant," I replied.

"I've put this little bureau desk in here if you want to do some of the work in your room. Otherwise, we'll work in the study which overlooks the field, so you can keep an eye on that big horse of yours. Now come into the kitchen, which is rather the hub of my house, and definitely the warmest room."

I followed her down the corridor. There was a drawing-room on the left, and I peeked inside and looked around. It had the air of a maiden aunt with chintzy furnishings and a distinct smell of damp. In comparison, the kitchen was very warm and cosy, and there was an enormous cream-coloured Aga from which emanated toasty warmth.

"Tea for two," she said with a hint of melody in the way she said it. Taking the kettle, she poured some hot water into the silver teapot to warm it, then three teaspoons of tea. Then opening a cake tin and bringing out the most luscious chocolate cake, with buttercream through the middle and thick chocolate icing on the top, she cut two slices, a very generous one for me and a thinner portion for herself.

"Here are the chapters that I've already written," she said, handing me a sheaf of papers which were sitting neatly on the kitchen table. It was certainly a substantial pile and handwritten. I cast my eye over them and saw to my intense relief it was legible. Having to decipher a spider's crawl would have been the most onerous and impossible of tasks!

I was so curious to read the manuscript that my large luscious slice of chocolate cake lay untouched on my plate! You can imagine just how much I needed to find out what my job was going to entail. I was determined to approach this task with unflagging zeal, so I started at the beginning and began to read.

There were some rather lyrical descriptions of Kenya with references to the landscape that painted a picture of colonial Africa: women dressed in furs, with long gloves, herds of long-necked giraffes, buffaloes, corrugated iron roofs, shooting safaris in tented camps with black Africans in white gloves serving dinner, gramophones playing music that competed with the sound of animals in the black velvet night, feathery thorn trees on river banks, intoxicating heat, silvery baobab trees, and sudden equatorial sunsets.

But these descriptive phrases leapt out at the reader for the bulk of the writing was in very plain language, simple sentence structures, not many adjectives or adverbs, factual to the core. I wondered whether I should try and jazz it up a bit with some catchy phrases, but I didn't know whether or not this was what she wanted, or should I simply type it up exactly as it had been written.

"Come, Jill, drink your tea and eat your cake," said Bryony breaking into my concentration.

"I'm sorry I was so interested."

"What if I tell you my history in shortened form, rather than reading pages and pages of detail that I know will have to be substantially reduced."

"Of course," I said.

She talked for half an hour while I sipped my tea and munched on the cake. I will try to summarise what she told me. She had been born in 1900 in England and had been a child during the first World War. Her father had died in the trenches, and then she and her mother had moved to London in

the 1920s. During the years between the wars, she had enjoyed an almost bohemian life in London, drinking coffee in cafes, smoking cigarettes in elegant cigarette holders, flirting with men and gossiping with friends. Then she had travelled to Kenya to work for a friend who trained polo ponies which was a popular sport there amongst the ex-patriots. At this point, I was sitting there with my mouth open. It sounded so exciting and my own life, which I thought was rather fascinating, seemed boring and tame in comparison.

Through her work there she came into contact with many of the socialites who had flocked to Kenya, often in exile for bad behaviour in England, or just to make their fortune and have adventures. She talked quite nonchalantly about members of the aristocracy with whom she had rubbed shoulders in Nairobi, and the social events she had attended at the Muthaiga Club.

Now I could go on and on, as Bryony did, but then this story would be about the estimable Mrs Peach and not about myself and my adventures. Just to satisfy you on one point which may have aroused your curiosity. Yes, she had been living in Kenya in 1940 when Lord Errol had been shot in the head in one of the most notorious murder mysteries of the century. She did believe she knew what had happened, and it hadn't been the rather pathetic Jock Delves-Broughton who had murdered him. But she assured me that this was going to be her story about her life and she would only write about her own actual interactions with Erroll, rather than prognosticate on the lives of others. She believed that this was simply courting sensationalism. I did wonder a little at the emphatic way in which she stated this as if there were a secret tale that she was afraid to tell.

We started work that very afternoon and Bryony began to dictate to me. I was a little slow but was able to decipher my own shorthand, and I would spend considerable time typing it up. Our days fell into a regular routine. We started work at nine o'clock in the morning with one hour of dictation, followed by two hours of typing. Then Bryony would serve me lunch, and we would discuss the notes I had written. She then dictated again from one o'clock until two o'clock.

Then I had a couple of hours respite to go and ride Balius. There was no area for schooling, but the surrounding countryside was beautiful, picturesque green fields with bridle paths and in the distance, I could see moorland. I enjoyed my riding enormously. The fresh air revived me from the rather intense secretarial duties.

I would return to the house for tea, more delicious cakes which Bryony bought hand-made in the village. I would spend another two hours typing,

and then supper. I would go to bed early, tired out by my secretarial labours and the good Cornish fresh air that blew in straight off the ocean.

I had been seduced by the luscious chocolate cake at that first afternoon tea. Unfortunately, this was the gastronomic highpoint of the day. Breakfast was toast, toast and more toast. Lunch was a cheese sandwich, and supper was a choice of frozen TV dinners ranging from lasagne, macaroni cheese, roast beef dinner, sweet and sour pork and whatever else the local supermarket was selling. Mummy had never approved of frozen meals, so, at first, it was rather a novelty but by the time I had tasted each of the types. I decided that home-cooked was best. I did offer to cook. Bryony's response was to thank me in a matter-of-fact tone but she said that there was absolutely no need for that and I should concentrate on the memoirs. So heated frozen dinners it was. The only good point about this arrangement was that it meant there wasn't much washing up.

Mr Bell brought his retired pony who was not at all sweet-tempered. He was a nasty little Shetland who encouraged Balius to run away from me the minute I turned up at the gate. If I didn't watch him, he would line me up and try and kick me. Rather annoyingly, Balius seemed to adore this horrid creature from hell. I would have thought that he should have had more discrimination in his affections.

The more I saw of the Cornish countryside, the more I loved it. Beautiful sea views, craggy rocky cliffs, a chequered pattern of green and gold fields, interspersed with chunky brown plough and even the occasional palm tree in Morrab Gardens in Penzance.

"I was thinking you must be rather missing the company of other young people," said Bryony one Saturday at breakfast. "I have invited my great-niece Jecca to come to dinner tonight. She is a few years older than you, but she also rides so you have a lot in common."

"That sounds good," I said a little hesitantly. Have you ever noticed that when someone says that you're going to get on well then that almost seals the deal and you will hate each other on sight.

"What sort of riding does she do?" I enquired politely.

"She used to do pony club, but these days I think she just goes out for rides on the moor. She doesn't compete or anything like that."

"Perhaps we can go riding together," I said rather less than hopefully, but it had been kind of Bryony to think of my welfare. I was finding that this shorthand and typing and to some extent editing, and re-writing were extremely arduous for my brain. In fact, it was more difficult than school had ever been! Much as I enjoyed writing my own stories, I was beginning to find that other people's stories were not nearly so enthralling. Not to say that I'm the most interesting and amusing person in the world but rather that the hardest part was being tactful. I made huge efforts to frame criticisms most politely, and this was more taxing than taking down shorthand. I know that Mummy often looks over my shoulder and puts a blue pencil through some of my writing, I longed to put my pencil through batches of pages, but I didn't have the necessary expertise or self-confidence. I did rather wonder what Mummy's publisher was going to make of it.

I was also finding that Bryony Peach morning, noon and night was just too intense. I do not doubt that she had led an interesting life, but the excruciating detail of one incident to the next was, quite frankly, doing me in. It was almost as if she were deliberately making it as dull as possible as if she rigorously filtered the story so that it was not at all interesting, no juicy gossipy details about the famous people that she mentioned. However, I couldn't just give up, I had agreed to do this job, and I would see it through, but, at the rate, we were going I thought we might need another whole lifetime to relive her original life. Although in theory, she had had a wonderful, colourful and dashing life, she seemed unable to translate this in writing, and her focus was on the mundane rather than the interesting.

Bryony had some rather extraordinary mannerisms that I also found extremely irritating. She would pause mid-sentence and pull her nose thoughtfully, and there would be a hush as I waited for the next long and convoluted idea. At night I was bashing away at the typewriter working on the chapters she had written out by hand until my fingers ached and the air rang with my muttered oaths.

The idea of a great-niece was at least a distraction. There was hope that we might get on as she also rode. She arrived in time for dinner, and immediately I sensed tension in the air. She was very suspicious of me and what I was doing here, asking me very detailed questions. Bryony was dismissive.

"Why Jecca, you know perfectly well that Jill has come to help me with my memoirs."

"But I could have done that for you," said Jecca, defensively.

"You don't have shorthand, and your typing is very slow. Whereas Jill is a fine little secretary."

I did think this was rather exaggerating my skills, and I had never envisaged myself as a 'fine little secretary'. But I wondered at Jecca's attitude. It was as if I was trying to steal her inheritance. A measly £15 per week I felt was only just adequate compensation for the efforts that I was making. What I found

especially irritating was Jecca's questioning about my daily routine and just how much work I did. I stifled my annoyance, and we grudgingly agreed that tomorrow she would meet me up on the moor at the signpost that pointed to Ding Dong Mine one way and St Buryan the other. I thought that perhaps she was going to use this as an opportunity to grill me once I was away from the protection of Bryony.

I rode Balius up there in the morning. One bright spot in my life was my beautiful horse, who was benefitting from the long, slow work every day and muscling up very satisfactorily. His manners had improved, and I found that he could work just as well on a loose rein, in self-carriage as with a gentle feel on his mouth. We practised various schooling movements such as from trot to halt, then trotting on. We also practised transitions from walk to canter and then to halt as we hacked along the narrow paths.

On this particular Sunday morning, there were great gusts of winds sweeping across the moor. I pulled my scarf more securely around my neck and felt grateful that Balius hadn't been clipped. It looked like it might rain at any minute. It wasn't the first time I'd ridden in Cornish storms, that blew up as quickly as they cleared. I could see the signpost in the distance, and as I approached, I saw another horse and rider coming from the direction of Madron, a small village near Penzance. It was Jecca mounted on a rather plain and ordinary cob. She rode quite well although I thought her feet too far forward and she sat back towards the cantle of the saddle.

"Hello!" I called in an insincere friendly voice.

"Hello," she said. "I do like that horse of yours, come on let's go over the moor I can show you the ruins of an old bronze age castle if you like. Also, there's a few old stone walls along the way we can jump."

I hadn't jumped Balius much anyway and certainly not since we had been to David Staley's yard. I didn't say anything. If she gave me a lead, I was certain that Balius would follow. I felt that Jecca was challenging me, and I was right. She took off at a smart canter, up the rocky track that twisted and turned. Obviously, the path was familiar to her horse. I hoped that Balius wouldn't fall down and break his knees.

We crossed what must have been a few old fields that were now overgrown, and I saw her horse jump ahead of me, what was really just a heap of rocks, a fallen down stone wall. I collected Balius and signalled to him that he had to pay attention, and he leapt neatly. I could feel the thrust of his hindquarters, and, again, I experienced that rush of hope that this horse had exceptional promise. We came to the top of the hill and then the rain came down, slanting like icy spears and hitting us in the face.

"I suppose we had better find somewhere to wait out the storm," said Jecca and she turned her horse around. I followed the cob's ample behind, and we made our way down to a tiny ruined farmhouse that nestled in the lee of the hill. It consisted of only three walls, but we were able to shelter from the worst of the rain.

"Do you like working for Bryony?" asked Jecca.

"It's alright, she's very kind," I said carefully. I was sure that anything I said would be reported back, probably misconstrued. I watched the skies wishing that it would clear. I didn't like being with Jecca. I sensed her dislike for me beneath the extremely thin veneer of politeness. To be honest, I'd been finding my existence hidden away in the valley rather lonely. It made Blainstock Castle seem like a hub of human activity.

Finally, the storm blew itself out and riding into the face of the last hissing arrows of icy rain Jecca took me back to the signpost where we had started. She rode off with hardly a word of farewell. She didn't suggest that we ride again and even though I didn't like her much I felt rejected. I was so used to hanging out with my bunch of jolly chums. I didn't quite know what to do in this lonely new world of serious grownup work. I rode back to the hidden valley feeling wet and uncomfortable and wishing I was back at the castle, luxuriating in a hot bath anticipating a savoury beef stew with thick gravy and dumplings. I was in the depths of depression and gloom. Life stretched before me - an endless round of shorthand, typing and reading over Bryony's life.

I had agonised over the memoirs for hours, and I thought that really half of it needed to be scrapped but I didn't feel that I had the professional skills to tell Bryony. She had been involved in several civil law cases, and she must have got the records from the Court, and these had been included almost word for word. Talk about absolutely deadly dull! Her idea to eschew all sensationalism was making what she wrote extremely boring.

"How did your ride go, Jill?" asked Bryony when I got back. This made me feel even worse for my uncharitable thoughts about her memoirs. She really was very kind-hearted.

"It was good," I said, "just need to go and change, I got a bit wet."

"I've cooked a meal myself," said Bryony proudly. "I thought you might appreciate something home-cooked."

"Whizzo," I said enthusiastically, "can't wait."

She had raised my hopes, and when she served it up, I just couldn't help my expression of horror. The mashed potato looked most unusual. Then, I

realised it was instant mash, and it tasted absolutely horrible. I piled on as much salt and pepper as possible and tried to force it down. The chicken was underdone, and there was blood swimming around the edge of the plate. I knew that if you didn't cook chicken well enough it could poison you and I was rather hoping to live to see the following day. I just couldn't bring myself to eat it. I didn't want to die before I got Balius to a competition.

"I'm terribly sorry, but I feel very sick, I've got the most awful stomach ache, it looks delicious, but I just can't eat it," I said lying through my teeth. I jumped up and upset my plate, and it splattered all over the floor. I rushed into the kitchen and found a rag to clean up the mess.

"Oh, my goodness, my golly gosh, I'm so sorry!" I said thinking at least there would be no question of me eating it now. I scrubbed away at the worn carpet, and then I went up to my room and lay down, I was going to have to do something. I didn't think I could manage much more of this food. I know this sounds extremely feeble, but as you know my dear readers - food is of great importance to me.

I had been here for eight weeks now, and that meant I had earnt £120, which was quite a substantial sum, but I certainly felt that I had worked hard for it. Unfortunately, Bryony seemed to be unflagging in her dictation efforts, and she was only thirty-two-years-old at this point, at least another thirty years to go! I just couldn't wriggle out of it. I had made a commitment and I had to stick to it.

I decided I would give Balius a day off the next day and spent my two hours off driving into Penzance. I would treat myself to a cooked meal and buy some provisions to augment my diet of toast, sandwiches and ready-cooked meals. I hadn't taken the Land Rover out since I'd arrived. It would do it good to have a run I only hoped that the battery hadn't gone flat.

It felt good to be driving out of the valley, and I only wished that I'd finished the job and was heading back to Scotland. I parked the Land Rover in Penzance and walked down the main street. There was a café called "The Copper Kettle" which served meals all day, and I went in and ordered a steak with salad. I was looking forward to crisp vegetables and real fresh meat. I sank my teeth into crunchy lettuce and then carved up the ribeye steak, utterly delicious, tender and very meaty. I felt like I had returned to the land of the living.

I was tempted to bolt down this delicious repast but exercised some self-control and ate as slowly as I could, trying to savour every mouthful. After I had paid the bill, I walked around town until I found a bookshop and went in. I saw that there was a special display of Mummy's books. I would have

to remember to tell her all about it in my next letter. I was very proud of her. I couldn't imagine that Bryony's memoirs were ever going to make it through to publication, let alone be showcased in any book shops.

I walked down to Mount's Bay and across the beach. The misty outline of the castle, St Michael's Mount, rose out of the grey sea, looking ghostly and romantic. The fresh air was blowing away my depression. Perhaps I should write to Mummy and explain to her the dilemma of the 'maudlin memoirs', and she could talk to the publisher. I did feel tempted to beg her to write and say that I was needed at home, so I could escape, but I knew that was not the right thing to do.

I walked back to the Land Rover and drove back to the valley. I felt bolstered up and determined to continue. I began to sing 'Onward Christian Soldiers' to build on this new mood. I would look at the latest chapter and see if I could make some editing suggestions that might improve it.

Chapter Eight – Running the Gauntlet

The next Saturday I was planning a long ride on Balius. I rose early and saddled up. I had made myself some cheese sandwiches and I had some money, and I was planning on getting all the way over to The Star Inn at St Just where I could have a Coca-Cola while sitting on the bench outside and holding Balius's reins. I was looking forward to some jolly chat with a few of the native inhabitants. Balius entered into the spirit of our adventure, and we made it all the way over the moors in record time, cantering along the narrow paths, nimbly skipping around jutting out rocks and filling ourselves with good fresh air. The pub was full, and some of the drinkers sat on the bench outside with me in the warm sunshine, and they chatted about local events. Reluctantly I mounted to ride back and arrived at the hidden valley when dusk was falling. I took Balius into the field and untacked him.

"Jill," whispered a voice. I nearly jumped out of my skin. Then I saw a figure emerge from the paddock shelter. It was Jecca.

"Oh, you gave me a fright," I said, "I nearly died of a heart attack."

"I need your help," she whispered melodramatically.

"Gosh you must be desperate," I said, thinking that I would have thought I was the last person she would ask for help.

"It's absolutely top secret, can I trust you?"

"Well, as long as it's not illegal," I said flippantly.

She didn't reply, and then I had a feeling that it might jolly well be illegal, and I didn't want to get dragged into this.

"Well it's a rescue mission, we have to save the dogs," she said.

"What on earth are you talking about?" I asked impatiently, but of course, she was appealing to the nobility in my nature that cared for all animals.

I picked up Balius's rug and threw it over him. I took his bucket of feed, already prepared, out from the back of the shed and tipped it into the manger.

"Can we go inside and talk?" I asked.

"No, I don't want Bryony to know anything about it. I know she won't approve."

I thought that I probably didn't approve either, but my curiosity was piqued. At last, something was happening to break the dreary and relentless routine of my days.

"We need you to drive us up to Devon tomorrow, in the Land Rover. You just drive. It's your day off. We'll pay you £50."

"£50!" I exclaimed.

"Sshhhh," she said. "You're hopeless. You've got no sense of adventure."

Well, that was like waving a red rag to a bull. As you readers will know I am the world's expert at adventures!

"I will have you know that I've had more adventures than you've had hot dinners," I retorted, and perhaps unwisely I added, "alright I'm up for it. When should we set off?"

"I'll meet you at the end of the lane down Bossiney Cove at six in the morning. It'll be me and my boyfriend. All you've got to do is drive us up to Devon. We'll pay for petrol and give you £50. You can tell Bryony you're off to visit some friends."

"You're on," I said. "I want to go inside it is freezing out here."

"OK, tomorrow."

I went inside. I felt sure that I should have asked more questions, but Jecca's melodramatic secrecy was extremely irritating, and I was longing for a hot cup of tea.

"Sorry I'm late," I said to Bryony.

"That's alright dear, a day out in the fresh air should do you good. I've left your dinner in the oven. It's lasagne."

"Great," I said, stifling a hollow groan. Another soggy, over-heated meal, full of preservatives and colouring. I poured on tomato ketchup, trying to make it more edible. To take my mind off the taste, I began to muse over this mystery trip - £50 was a ridiculous amount of money – what on earth was Jecca and this dubious boyfriend up to? To save the dogs, what could that mean? I guessed I would find out tomorrow. It would certainly boost my savings for a second horse. I wondered if I should write to Ned Sperrit and ask him whether he had found anything suitable for me yet.

I wrote a note that I would leave on the kitchen table for Bryony tomorrow, telling her I was off for the whole day and not to leave me any supper. I would treat myself to fish and chips somewhere along the way. Then I set my alarm for quarter past five, which would give me plenty of time to feed

Balius, have a cup of tea and drive to the meeting place. I was curious and suspicious in equal measures over this strange, secret mission. I would make them explain immediately, and if it really was illegal, then I would refuse to take part.

The weather was not conducive to secret missions, or so I thought. It was pouring rain. The road had streams of water running down it. But on the other hand, perhaps it was the best weather for surreptitious behaviour. No-one would be out and about unless it was absolutely necessary. It was staying-at-home-in-bed weather. I drove down to Bossiney Cove, and Jecca was huddled in a raincoat in the bus shelter. She jumped into the Land Rover and told me to drive as if the enemies were after us.

"No way," I said firmly. I turned the engine off and sat there. "You tell me what this is about or we're not going anywhere!"

She looked like she was about to scream, and I wondered if she would knock me out and steal the car.

"I'll tell you the truth, and then you'll understand that this is the right thing to do."

"The whole truth," I said firmly.

"My boyfriend, Dean, he has this business that he does. Well, he's part of it. It's about bringing dogs over from Europe on the boats, so they don't have to go through quarantine."

I sat there thinking, my knowledge of quarantine law was pretty sketchy.

"I don't understand," I said.

"If you bring a dog over from the Continent, then he has to go into six months' quarantine, even if he's had all his jabs and a vet certificate, and it's cruel. The dogs hate quarantine, horrid little cement cells, and they just don't understand why they are there. So, Dean's friends bring them over in boats and then he delivers them to their owners."

"OK, so that's why it is illegal," I said slowly, my thoughts running like rats around a wheel trying to work out whether this was right or wrong. It did seem to be much kinder for the dogs, and if they'd had their injections, then there was no danger.

"So, what is the big emergency now?" I asked.

"The Customs and Excise men are watching his place. We think they're about to swoop. So, Dean sneaked the dogs out two nights ago, and they've been up on the moor, and I've been taking them food. But we've got to get

them back to their owners. We can't risk them going up in Dean's car in case the police stop him."

Now I understood the urgency and the offer of £50.

"This £50 you're going to pay me, that seems a lot," I said. If I took the money, then I wouldn't be able to say I did it as a mission of mercy. I would be involved in a sordid illegal activity. On the other hand, it was such a gorgeous amount of money, and it could go towards my second horse. Typing and shorthand at £15 per week wasn't adding up very quickly. I saw that the road to criminality was tempting, the offer of lucrative profits. This might well be the thin end of the wedge.

"Where do we have to deliver the dogs?" I asked, deciding that I would, just this once, throw in my lot with the baddies.

"Two of them are in Devon, and the other one is Somerset."

I thought about this for about twenty seconds.

"Come on. We have to hurry, two nights up on the moor is doing those dogs no good. They're pedigree, you know, very valuable dogs," urged Jecca.

This tipped me over the edge. The dogs were in distress, and I was helping to get them home.

"Let's go then," I said. "Are you sure the police won't be intercepting us along the way."

"How can I be sure?" asked Jecca, her voice high-pitched with annoyance. It looked like we were running the gauntlet and I was going to have to earn this money.

"Alright, I agree, let's get going and pick up the pooches," I said gaily. "It must be cold up on that moor."

"I'll tell you where to go," said Jecca.

We went to Newbridge, a small hamlet situated halfway across the moor towards St Just. Jecca directed me down a rough, rutted lane and there by an old falling down gate was a tall, lean young man wearing a full-length oilskin. He had three dogs on leads. There was a big one and two small ones, and they looked extremely bedraggled. Jecca jumped out and opened the rear door, and he climbed in the back, and she picked up the dogs and placed them inside with him. Then she ran back around to the cabin and got in and sat beside me.

"Let's go. You can turn a bit further up. We need to get out of here."

There were no other vehicles on the road, and I kept a keen eye on the side mirror, but no-one was following us. I felt a delicious thrill run through me; this was life, with a capital "L". This was an adventure worthy of an Enid Blyton story. Although possibly the Famous Five would have been on the tail of the dog smugglers to capture them. The lines between right and wrong were getting rather blurry at this point.

"Straight over and onto the A30 and up the country to Devon," said Jecca. She pulled a couple of towels out of her rucksack and handed them over. Then she pulled out a box of Bonios and gave it to the boyfriend to give to the dogs. The boyfriend had long hair which hung about his face in uncombed hanks, and it was hard to see what he looked like. It was probably better than I didn't know.

"The dogs are all wet and shivering," she said.

Dean didn't say a word. He was obviously the strong, silent type. I wondered whether I shouldn't ask for the £50 upfront but decided not to stir the pot.

"Do you know how to get there, this first dropping-off place?" I asked.

Jecca looked at Dean who must have nodded. I settled down to drive, concentrating on the road, which was rather treacherous in these weather conditions. Dean was ministering to the dogs in the back, and I glanced at him in the rear-view mirror from time to time. He was gentle with them; they certainly hadn't been ill-treated. I was dying to know who they belonged to and what dire circumstances had led to them being smuggled, but I sensed that Dean was the uncommunicative type. I didn't like this silence. I'm one to fill any gaps with a stream of chatter.

"Bryony tells me that you are a vegetarian, Jecca?" I said conversationally, not repeating what Bryony had really said which was that Jecca was a 'mung bean'.

"What's it to you," she snapped back at me.

"I was just trying to make conversation," I replied defensively. "We've got a long way to drive, and this awkward silence is getting on my nerves! I don't think that I've ever met a vegetarian before."

Jecca seemed a little mollified but still suspicious that I was being critical.

"It's Dean who showed me how good it is. You know the dogs are also on vegetarian diets."

I opened my mouth like a goldfish at this, but I could feel Dean glowering at the back of my head, so I swallowed down my obvious retort that surely dogs were carnivores!

"Sorry, it's just that we're a bit edgy," said Jecca, "it's a huge fine if we get caught."

I was assuming that she meant the fine was for smuggling the dogs rather than force-feeding them a vegetarian diet.

"Well, that makes me feel better," I said dryly.

"How do you think they got onto you?" I asked.

"We think it might have been one of the neighbours. They'd come over and noticed that there were at least half a dozen dogs in the kennels and commented on it," replied Dean.

"Does that mean this is the end of your business?" I asked.

"Certainly, the end of keeping dogs in that location," said Jecca.

We drove on, and I decided that silence was preferable. I was pretty sure that we weren't being followed, so I hoped we weren't going to get caught. If worst came to worst, I would just say I was giving these two a lift and as far as I knew they were Dean's dogs. This would entail lying to the Customs and Excise men, or the police, or whoever it was that investigates these things, and it was not something that I thought I would ever do. Mummy would have been quite horrified.

"We need fuel," I said when we came to Bodmin. I drove into a garage and asked the attendant to fill it up.

"Here's the money to pay for your fuel," said Dean gruffly. It was the first time he had spoken. "And, here's your fifty quid," he said, handing over a roll of dirty £5 notes.

I hesitated before I took it. This would seal my fate as a criminal, and I wasn't sure if I wanted it on my conscience. Then a vision of a beautiful chestnut gelding, leaping over six-foot fences floated before my eyes, and I took the money. I paid for the fuel and stuffed the rest in my jacket pocket. There was no looking back. I felt like I would be robbing banks at gunpoint by next week. I was on a slippery slope.

"We have to head for a place near Great Torrington," said Jecca, consulting a hand-written piece of paper.

"If we get stopped, I guess you eat that piece of paper," I said jokingly.

"Ha, ha!" she retorted sarkily. I could see exactly what she was thinking, that I was an absolute square and I didn't mind at all, I was never ever going to be like these two!

"For goodness sake, keep your sense of humour," I said sharply.

The rain had ceased, and the sky was lightening. Sunlight always cheered me up. I began to enjoy this adventure. I reasoned that we were actually doing good, helping these poor dogs and their devoted owners. Obviously, the quarantine laws were not sensible. The dogs in the back had settled down now, and Dean was brushing their coats. I began to whistle.

We were approaching Great Torrington, and Jecca began to direct me here and there around a seemingly convoluted route of tiny lanes. I wondered if she was just trying to confuse me, so I wouldn't know where we had been. She certainly succeeded, and I merely followed her directions. Then we stopped in a layby. There were no houses in sight, and I imagined that my two partners in crime were being ultra-careful. Jecca got out and opened the rear door for Dean. He took one of the smaller dogs. He led him to a public footpath that was signposted off the layby, tucking the squirming little creature beneath his arm as he climbed the stile and disappeared.

"Now drive on about a mile and then head back on a lane to the left," said Jecca.

"You're pretty good at finding your way," I said admiringly.

"I was in the girl guides," she said. I wasn't sure whether she meant it or was being facetious. I began to think that if these were doggy people, then I preferred horsey ones.

Dean came loping back down the road.

"It's all cool," he said quickly, as he leapt in. "Now we're heading for Withypool!"

"Oh Withypool," I cried in delight. "That's where Mousie lived."

"Who?" asked Jecca suspiciously.

"Oops," I said light-heartedly. "Just a pony," I replied dismissively.

"We need to head across to Exmoor along one of these smaller roads," said Jecca, tracing her finger on the map.

"I've never been to Exmoor," I said conversationally, "but I was staying with this lovely family on Dartmoor, on my way down to Cornwall."

Jecca looked at me, and I could almost hear what she was thinking, that she wished I'd go straight back to where I came from. I couldn't really understand why she was like this. I had never done anything to hurt her; perhaps it was just one of the vagaries of nature.

The sun was shining brightly now, and I pretended to myself that we were on a holiday jaunt. At least this adventure had broken the tedium of secretarial duties. I was getting a little tired and rather hungry.

"Can we stop for something to eat?" I asked.

Jecca and Dean looked at each other as if fearing that my request was a trap.

"I'm hungry," I said very slowly as if trying to explain to aliens from outer space who didn't understand simple human motivation.

"When we get to Withypool, you and Jecca can go into one of the cafes and have a meal. I'll make my way to the owner's place. She's expecting us. Don't expect me to pay for your grub," said Dean gruffly.

The drive seemed endless, but along the way, I spotted a herd of wild ponies grazing across the hill on the left-hand side of the road.

"Look, ponies!" I shouted, forgetting that my fellow travellers were not at all interested in anything horsey. Nonetheless, I drew over to the side of the road and turned off the Land Rover and pocketed the key, just in case they stole the vehicle and left me stranded! I walked slowly up the slope, trying to blend into the landscape. I got quite close to the ponies. I suppose they were used to people approaching them.

They all had mealy noses as if their muzzles had been dipped in a mixture of cayenne pepper and yellow turmeric. They were absolute darlings. I stood still and watched them nosing around in the heather looking for the bright green young shoots of grass that were springing up. Three of the mares were very heavy with foals, and I thought it wouldn't be long before there would be a clutch of fluffy-tailed bundles of joy dancing and frolicking in the purple ling. By the time it was high summer they would lie down under the shade of the stunted ancient oak trees that grew in the deep combes. Honeysuckle would wreathe the branches and flavour the air with a heavy fragrant sweet smell. I went off into a pony-dream inspired by this vision that I had read in the Mousie books. Then I heard a shout from the Land Rover.

"For God's sake, hurry up, we've got no time to be looking at the sights!" shouted Jecca, her voice rough-edged with anger.

"Alright, alright. You could have let the pooches have a bit of a run," I said irritably. My fellow smugglers were getting on my nerves.

I could hear my stomach growling with hunger. On we drove, and eventually we crossed the stone bridge over the River Barle and pulled up outside the tea rooms. By this time, I was faint with hunger and wondered if I would manage to totter in.

"I'll take this dog, perhaps you can sit in the garden with the other one, give him some fresh air," said Dean

I shrugged and dived through the door. I needed food. Jecca could see to the dog.

I ordered roast beef sandwiches, and if I hadn't been so hungry, I would have shared the roast beef with the poor deprived dog. I couldn't imagine what sort of people wouldn't let dogs eat meat. Then I thought I did know what sort of people, these 'beatnik' types with their floppy clothes and weirdo ideas. I turned back to the task of filling my starving tummy and ordered two huge scones loaded with strawberry jam and clotted cream and a big pot of tea. I imagined that this might be the last food stop until we got back to Cornwall.

I gobbled my food down in a most unladylike manner. Dean had told us to wait, and he was taking ages. Jecca began to fret. Perhaps she thought the Customs and Excise had been waiting for him. Eventually, he slunk up and stood lounging beside the Land Rover. We all climbed back in.

"Where to now?" I asked in a jovial manner. These two really were blots, not a smile between them. I decided that the alternative lifestyle wasn't much fun if you became this miserable. They seemed to take themselves very seriously.

"We head up towards Somerset, then it's near Burnham-on-Sea," said Jecca.

I began to whistle again, anything to break the solemn silence. There was only one dog left, and when it was delivered, presumably we were home and clear. I was getting weary, and I wasn't sure I'd be able to stay awake all the way back. But it was Richard's Land Rover, and I didn't think I should let Dean drive. When we got to the seaside town, which was famous for its muddy beach that stretched for miles when the tide was out, I went and bought a coffee trying to keep myself awake.

We decided to risk it and drove just a house or two beyond the delivery point. Dean was in and out, and then we were heading south again to Cornwall. I drove, and I drove and decided that I could never be a truck driver, as it was so boring after a while. I felt like I was crossing possibilities off my list rather than thinking of an occupation for myself. I quite liked taking down shorthand and rattling away on the typewriter was rather fun when I was writing my own books. The only thing I really liked was riding. I didn't mind doing stable duties but being a groom for the rest of my life looking after other people's horses wasn't going to be much fun either. Perhaps as Mummy and Richard faded away and retired, then I could take over the shooting season guests at the castle. That I did enjoy! Entertaining, but not the shooting!

Eventually, we got back, and I drove into Penzance to drop Jecca and Dean who were sneaking down the back streets to stay with friends, who were no doubt also weird vegetarian types. I imagined them sitting around a casserole of lentils and beans and plotting more anti-establishment plans. I pulled up outside the chippie and bought myself a generous portion of fresh fried fish and chips. I ate it as I drove.

I arrived back at the hidden valley at Lamorna. There were no Customs and Excise or police waiting to pounce on me, and I staggered out to check Balius and then went inside and fell asleep on my bed with my clothes on. A life of crime was no soft option. Utterly exhausting!

Chapter Nine – Intrigue and Murder

To me, this smuggling adventure was huge and on the scale of a grand international crime. I was a little uneasy about the morality of it but decided that as a one-off, it was relatively harmless. However, I felt a little nervous and found myself watching out the window, wondering whether Customs and Excise men were going to descend at any moment to drag me off in handcuffs and interrogate me.

By Wednesday, I was beginning to relax and breathe easily. I spent the day taking down shorthand and then typing in the usual routine. We were up to Christmas 1940, and Bryony was enjoying a wonderful life in Kenya, training polo ponies, drinking at the Muthaiga Club and living in a world that was a long way away from wartime Britain in the grip of the Blitz. Sometimes she would pause and look away into the distance, presumably back down through the years to a life, when the sun was always shining. I knew that Josslyn Hay, the Earl of Erroll had been murdered in January 1941 and I was hoping that there was going to be some sort of revelation that would make this book ground-breaking. I can only say to you readers, be careful what you wish for as it may come true!

I rode Balius in the afternoon, and we walked down to the cove and into the waves so that his legs could benefit from saltwater. We walked up and down the cold foamy water swirling about beneath us. The air was warm, and the sun a little brighter. I was looking forward to the summer, but rather hoping that I might be back in Scotland soon.

Dinner was excruciatingly awful, some type of fish pie that was glutinous and tasteless. I forced it down as I didn't want to starve. I went to bed and fell asleep but woke with a horrid start. Bryony was standing over me, gently shaking me.

"What is it?" I asked, leaping up, thinking that the Customs and Excise must be banging on the door, coming after me.

"Jill, I'm so sorry to wake you, but I must talk to you. I don't know what to do. Perhaps you'll have some ideas."

I thought this was rather a big ask. Bryony had lived many years and always gave the impression of being in command of herself and very organised. This seemed a very strange thing for her to say.

"What is it?" I asked.

"It's the memoirs. Poor Joss is about to be murdered. You know he was shot at point-blank range while he was driving his car back to Nairobi in the early

hours of the morning. And you see I have a pretty good idea of what happened but if I tell I believe that my life might be in danger."

"Oh, my golly gosh!" I gasped. This was not at all what I was expecting. "Do you think the murderer might come after you?"

"No, it's not that, you see it might be treason. I believe that was the real reason that Joss was murdered, because of his politics and what he knew."

"Well, all I know is what you've told me, and he was a patriot, he believed in England, the Empire and he was very involved in the local war activities," I said slowly, trying to gather my thoughts.

"Yes, I know, but he was mixed up with those aristocrats before the war, and he had joined up with the British Union of Fascists, you know led by Oswald Mosley."

"My knowledge of all that is pretty sketchy," I said thinking that the history that we had learnt at school hadn't ever touched on the subject of the British fascists who had known Hitler and supported him before the war. I had heard that Diana Mitford had been interned in prison for the duration of several years, and she had been married to Oswald Mosley, but beyond that, I was clueless.

"Tell me what you know," I said, perhaps a little reluctantly. The last thing I wanted to do was get involved in some ghastly anti-government intrigue that made dog-smuggling look like a harmless hobby!

"You see there was this woman, she had been riding at the polo club, taking a horse out every morning, and I know that she was involved with Joss. Sometimes I saw them talking, their heads together. Well, this was nothing new, he was always consorting with one woman or another even though things with him and Diana Broughton were sizzling hot at that time, although I don't think he was really the philanderer that he was known as. I think that was part of the plot you see, to make out that every husband in Kenya wanted to kill him. To divert attention from the real plot."

"The real plot," I echoed, rather incredulously. I was finding it a little hard to follow her line of reasoning.

"Yes, you see I think that this woman was a spy, an assassin, and the British government had arranged for her to kill him. You see the British fascists had had links with the previous King. You know the one that had to abdicate for marrying that American divorcée."

"Do you actually have any evidence?" I asked, my voice had now dropped to a whisper as if the walls had ears.

"Not absolute total evidence but you see there were a few strange things going on at the time, and I guess I put two and two together and came up with this rather hare-brained theory."

"Have you told anyone else about this?" I asked, feeling totally out of my depth. I had a nightmarish vision of us being assassinated by the Government secret services.

"There were whispers in Kenya. Although they arrested poor old Jock Delves-Broughton it just didn't seem to add up."

"So, now you're wondering if you should include these 'strange events' in the memoirs?" I said, trying to frame the problem clearly.

"Yes, I've been thinking about it a lot, ever since I started this project and I knew that I was going to have to make a decision."

"You know this is far too big for me to understand," I said apologetically.

"Yes, I'm sorry, you're really only a child," she said. "Well I don't mean that in an insulting way, you're very young and how could you possibly understand about these things."

"Why don't you go up to London and talk to your publisher, I know that whenever Mummy comes to an impasse in her writing, she says that he has a wonderfully sharp mind and can see right through to the core of the thing."

"Yes, you're right. I do believe that he is a trustworthy sort of man. That he could advise me and see a way through this."

I breathed a huge sigh of relief. This was all too big and dastardly for my somewhat innocent young mind to grapple with.

"Why don't we go into the kitchen and have a cup of tea," I suggested, thinking that poor Bryony must have been carrying around these dark thoughts for many years.

I put on my dressing gown and slippers, and we went down into the kitchen. I got out the cake tin with the chocolate cake. Even if Bryony was too upset to eat, I felt in need of a large slice to sustain me through the night. I poured her a cup of tea and got her to drink it with an extra spoonful of sugar.

"Why don't you tell me what you know?" I suggested, "just to get it off your chest. I promise I will never tell a soul or betray you, but perhaps you need to say it out loud."

The story she told me was absolutely stupendous, but I have to keep my word, and I can't repeat it, so my dear readers, you will merely have to imagine what happened according to the clues that I have given you.

It was as if my small foray into the illegal world of smuggling had jolted my universe and all sorts of strange things began to occur. Bryony wrote a letter to her publisher, and he rang her as soon as he received it. He insisted that she go to London, so they could discuss it seriously and confidentially.

Bryony suggested that perhaps I might like to finish up. She thanked me sincerely for all the help I had given her but said that she might make other arrangements, depending upon what was decided by herself and her publisher. She paid me in cash what I was owed with a little extra as a bonus. So, I had £150 from her, my £50 illegal earnings and about £150 left of my savings. This came to the princely sum of £360 and if you doubled that with Richard's promise to contribute as much as I had, then I could buy a horse that cost £700. I drove Bryony to the train station and waved her off, and the first thing on my agenda was a phone call to Ned Sperrit to see if he had found me a horse.

I talked to his sister, who promised to give him a message, but I wasn't sure that she really would, she didn't seem very helpful. I hopped around from one foot to another. It was April now, Easter next week and spring did come early in Cornwall. Swathes of daffodils nodded their heavy heads along the roadside. I took Balius out for a long ride, and we went around the coast to Marazion, and I galloped him along the beach. I was impatient to move on. My sojourn in Cornwall was coming to an end. When we returned to the house, the phone was ringing. It was Ned. My heart leapt. I was sure that he had found me the perfect horse.

"Hello, young Jill," he said. I very nearly replied, 'Hello old Ned' but stopped myself just in time.

"Have you found my horse for me?" I asked.

"Well funny you should ask, but I think I might 'av."

"Really! Golly gosh! I don't believe it!" I exclaimed.

"Now, don't get too excited. I found her last week, and she's not looking too clever at the moment, but I've been doing some investigating, and I know her, she's certainly seen some better times."

"Oh," my heart sank. It sounded like a rescue. Not that I'm against rescuing poor animals who have fallen into desperate circumstances, but I wanted something ready-made that I could get on and go out and compete.

"Tell me what you mean?" I asked.

"Well, if she's the horse I think she is then she would be about fourteen and she's been badly neglected, malnourished, like she wasn't looked after, but I remember her. She has a quite distinctive marking, a splash of white on

her belly like she stepped in a paint tin, crooked white blaze and four white socks."

"She sounds striking, but how tall?"

"Well, she's not as big as that grey chap you've got, possibly 15.3 hh, perhaps a shade over just under 16 hh."

"Do you know what she's done?"

"I can't be certain, but if she's the mare I think, she was a top little showjumper and also clocked up some wins in the lightweight hack classes. I think she used to belong to young Ophelia Nettlebed. I'm going to ring old man Nettlebed tonight and see what has happened to this mare if it is her, her name was Copperplate. It's that splash of white on her belly that makes me think it's her. Now the thing is she doesn't look good I need a few weeks to get some condition on her. She looks a sight right now."

"You see I think I'm heading back to Scotland tomorrow or the day after. I don't mind what she looks like. I want to see her."

"I'll ring you when I know if it really is her and find out what happened."

I hung up. With this, I had to be content. I wanted to drive straight up and see her. I believed I was enough of a horsewoman to be able to discern a good horse no matter what their condition. I thought about the names - Ophelia Nettlebed and Copperplate. It did sound vaguely familiar if only I was at Blainstock I could go through the piles of *Horse and Hound* magazines and see if there was any mention of them.

I was restless, the house was empty, and I felt as if I were hanging in a vacuum. I wanted action. Then I realised that I hadn't even asked Ned the cost of the mare, but then perhaps that depended on what he found out about her.

I rang Blainstock and talked to Mummy, telling her that Bryony had gone to London and I planned to be setting out on my journey north in a day or two. Bryony then rang to tell me that Jecca would be turning up to housesit, and she asked me to contact Mr Bell so he could come and take back his ferocious bad-tempered little pony.

So, my employment drew to a halt with a minimum of fuss. I smiled to myself thinking that the house in the hidden valley would no doubt be the half-way stop for smuggled dogs and I was glad to be out of it. I decided that I'd had my one experience of skating along on the wrong side of the law and I wouldn't be doing that again! Now Jecca had no reason to be jealous of me, she could be the queen of the hidden valley, and I would gladly skedaddle back to Scotland.

I rang the Merrivales first and asked if I could stay one night on my way up and then I hoped I could drive right through to Ned Sperrit's place to see the chestnut mare. I rang much later that night when I was sure he would be in, and he told me I could stay the night when I turned up. He was still investigating the little mare, but at least I could see her. I got off the phone, and I was leaping around like a jackrabbit, beside myself with excitement. Of course, those of you who know horses will say that this is no attitude to approach the buying of a new horse, that one must reserve judgement, look around, get a vet check and preferably a week's trial but I just knew, deep in my heart that she was the one.

I threw my clothes into my bag and packed all of the horse equipment into the Land Rover and hooked on the trailer and positioned it in the driveway ready to drive away early the next morning. Jecca was to arrive mid-morning, so I wouldn't even wait for her to arrive. I would be straight up to the Merrivales.

Chapter Ten – Leaving Cornwall

Everything went according to plan. I was driving up the A30 by seven o'clock in the morning. As I wheeled along, I suddenly remembered Badminton. Presumably, Mark would be going. I couldn't remember the exact dates, but it must be about now. With any luck, he would be away when I arrived back and then life would be perfect. Especially if I was to bring my new mare with me. I hoped that Balius and she would get on if they were to travel together. I would tie them up short, so they didn't have enough room to bite at each other. I gave myself a good talking to, I was assuming that I was definitely going to buy the mare, and this was not at all professional.

The Merrivales were gratifyingly pleased to see me. All the kids leapt about asking for details of my time in Cornwall, begging me to stay an extra day as they had planned a huge ride with a picnic. In the end, they persuaded me. I decided that all this rush to see an unknown mare was a little ridiculous if it prevented me from enjoying a fabulous day out with these wonderful people. One more day wouldn't make any difference, and it was such a relief to be surrounded by truly horsey and happy people. We chattered away ten to the dozen talking about their ponies. I asked them about Copperplate and Ophelia Nettlebed, but they had never heard of them. They knew everyone in their small corner of England but not many beyond that.

I rang Ned Sperrit for just three minutes and told him to expect me not the next day but the one after. He sounded very quiet, and I sensed there was something he wasn't telling me. I suddenly felt hugely let down. Perhaps he had found another buyer. I reasoned with myself there were plenty of horses for sale, I could check through the advertisements in *Horse and Hound* and the local papers, and I could write to Wendy at the riding school where I had learnt to ride. I had to live in the moment and tomorrow would be a gorgeous day with my bunch of new friends with such a jolly outing, after all these weeks of riding just Balius and me on the bleak, empty moors.

It was a fantastic day, and the ponies were bright-eyed and full of joy, they could snuff the warm breezes of the coming summer. Balius kicked up his back feet when we had our first canter. He seemed to sense the joy and excitement in the air. The Merrivales took me around the moor to a place where they had built up some of the falling-down stone walls into a type of a course. I tucked in behind them, and the ponies all jumped confidently, and Balius followed without a second thought. I was filled with happiness.

"Now let's go around one by one," suggested Olly.

"That's a brilliant idea, and we can time each other," said Sandy.

We stood in a bunch at the top of the hill, and the course of five stone walls spread out below us, up one hill and down the other, then a final leap over a fast-running stream and between two bushes that were designated the finish.

As it was Olly's idea, he went first. This was obviously not his first attempt at the course, and he careered round very, very quickly, his pony leaping and twisting in the air as it landed and headed for the next obstacle. They suggested that as the visitor, I should go next. There was no way I was going for a fast time. I would have no chance of beating these little moorland-bred ponies anyway. I trotted down the hill and then looked up to the others. Sandy raised her arm and dropped it. We were off, and Balius cantered steadily towards the first wall, it was perhaps only two feet high and two feet wide, but he pricked his ears, and a stride away increased his pace and popped over. He jumped each wall as if he were a seasoned hunter.

"Not bad!" shouted Sandy as I trotted back up the hill. "You were only seven seconds behind Olly. Each of the others jumped the course, and I was particularly impressed by Buttons and his diminutive little black pony. They went around as if they were racing in the Grand National. Olly was the eventual winner and needless to say I was last, but I didn't mind, my heart was singing at the way Balius had tackled this first impromptu competition.

We rode on and eventually reached a clump of rocks that formed a natural circle. The Merrivales had obviously been here before, and the gaps in the rocks were stacked with old gorse. We rode into the centre and pulled branches across the opening, and it was a secure pen for the ponies to be let loose. We untacked them and let them free. I was a little nervous that Balius might decide to jump out and gallop off, but he was very happy to hang out with his little mates. We investigated our saddlebags that Mrs Merrivale had packed with the most delicious food, and we sat on the sun-warmed rocks and looked out at the view, rolling slopes with flashes of green and purple, the grey and brown landscape of winter was being renewed.

After lunch, we lay down on the rocks and soaked up the sunshine. The Merrivales were full of plans for the summer. They had decided to go trekking for ten days with a pack pony they were borrowing from a neighbour. They had planned the route riding all the way to the sea.

"You could come with us, Jill. It is going to be the most tremendous fun. We haven't quite persuaded the parents, but I'm sure with you being nearly a grown-up, well technically, but not in spirit! Then that will reassure them no end."

"It sounds wonderful," I said musing over the idea. I could bring Balius down in the horse trailer, and it would be the most blissful fun. I could even suggest to Richard that we could start running a few treks up at Blainstock and this jaunt would be something in the way of research into a new business idea.

"Alright, I'm in," I said. "I don't suppose I could bring a friend?"

"Why not, the more the fun and two nearly grown-ups would be even more reassuring for the parents," said Sandy.

"That's sorted then. We can talk to your parents tonight and perhaps make a date."

We caught the ponies and Balius and saddled up and rode home slowly. We chattered on and on, making plans, imagining scenarios and adventures that might befall us on the best pony trek in Ponydom as the Merrivales called it.

I entertained them with the story of how I had once wished that I lived in Ecuador, where I could have pony trekked every day of my life. Since then, one of my friends from school had been to Ecuador and told me that they ate guinea pigs, baked whole, cut in half with all the innards and garnished with a green pea sauce. They all agreed that this sounded like the most disgusting of all meals and we all declared that pony trekking on Dartmoor would be a hundred times better.

On the way back to the farm house, I regaled the Merrivales with tales of the one and only pony trek I had ever undertaken, which I had written about in one of my books. I had them all roaring with laughter.

Then they showed me the Coffin Stone.

"What is the story connected to this?"

"The legend says that there was a very, very evil man who died and his coffin was being carried to the Widecombe Churchyard for burial. Dartmeet Hill is a steep climb, so they put the coffin on the stone for a rest on the way up. They believed that God was so angry that such a bad man was to be buried in sanctified ground that a massive thunderbolt was sent to earth and destroyed the coffin and split the earth."

"Wow, that is freaky," I exclaimed. "What had the evil man done to be so evil?"

We then spent ten minutes making up stories about a totally evil man. It was such fun to be with young people whose imaginations were as lively as my own. Olly concluded this discussion with the statement.

"You know I think we live in the spookiest place in England!"

"Isn't it just brilliant here!" exclaimed Rosie with a wide smile splitting her face.

"It's not just the spooks and the ghosts there are peat bogs that suck you under in a minute and don't leave a trace!" said Posy.

"When we go on the pony trek we'll take you on a ghostly trail," said Buttons.

I began to wonder then whether it wasn't all a trick to try and scare me out of my wits. Even so, it sounded absolutely fascinating, and I believed that I was a stout-hearted person when it came to ghosts and ghoulies, they wouldn't scare me that easily!

Over supper, the children told their parents about the plan that I should come with them, and possibly one of my friends. Mr and Mrs Merrivale were quite reassured at this idea. I told them it would have to be organised right at the beginning of the holidays as I had to be back at the castle several days before the Glorious Twelfth, when the shooting season began, and we were all in the thick of entertaining our guests and their children.

I set my alarm for very early the next day. I had an absolutely massive three hundred miles to drive to get to Preston. Although I could have chosen to break my journey along the way and even stop at Cheltenham at Charles and Venetia's I felt a little shy at just ringing them and asking if I could come and stay, they were so impossibly glamorous. It wasn't the same as asking the Merrivales. I had chosen two places along the way when I would stop and let Balius have a crop at the roadside and drink some water and have a walk around. I couldn't wait to get to Ned Sperrit's to see Copperplate.

I drove off early in the morning full of a huge portion of fried bacon rashers and eggs done perfectly with soft yolks and mushrooms and fried bread. I felt as if I had eaten enough for the whole day. Mrs Merrivale had also pressed upon me a big packet of sandwiches, home-made biscuits and three apples. No matter what I wasn't going to starve.

We drove and drove and drove and came to the large grassy parkland where I had planned to take Balius out for a break. I let down the ramp and went inside the trailer and untied him and unpinned the rear bar. As he backed

out, I reached for the lead rope that I had carefully looped over his neck. Then at that exact moment, a dog bounded out of nowhere and yapped vociferously at his heels. Balius flung his head up, and I slipped on the ramp, and he was away. This was my worst nightmare. In the middle of nowhere near the main road, no-one to help my precious horse and me loose in a panic.

"Balius! Balius!" I called trying not to screech. I had to remain calm and confident. But it was too late. His tail in the air like a banner, high-stepping like a circus horse, he did this floating-in-the-air trot across the park towards the trees in the distance. I took a deep breath, so I wouldn't have a panic attack. Then I took a bucket and put in some oats.

I ran a dozen or so steps, so I didn't lose sight of him altogether. Then I remembered that I'd left the Land Rover unlocked with all my gear in it. Should I go back and lock up, or risk it and keep going after him. I decided that rescuing Balius before he ran into an oncoming truck was more important. I walked steadily towards him. Then I saw him swerve and canter at an angle as if heading back for the road. I changed direction.

"Balius! Balius!" I called, but he seemed not to hear me, or perhaps not to care.

I felt like I was about to cry, and I hated that, I hated the idea of being a cry-baby. I had to be strong, but I had a vision of him lying in a heap on the road, crushed and bleeding, and I would arrive as he gasped his last breath.

Some young boys ran up to me and cried out.

"Miss, we'll help you catch him!"

"We'll surround him!"

They began to pelt after him, and I knew that this was disastrous. This was the last thing one should do in such a situation.

"Stop! Stop!" I shouted at them. Fortunately, they heard me and did as I asked.

"We need to keep him away from the road, but if you chase him, then that will make him worse. Fan out along in that direction and head him off if he goes towards the road, but quietly, calmly, don't get him more excited."

There were four of them, and they seemed to be bright lads, and they did as I asked. Balius was still trotting along, looking around. The four boys ran away from Balius and then got to the road and walked back towards him, to head him off. Then he started trotting back towards me.

"Just stand still!" I shouted to the boys.

"Balius! Balius!" I called rattling the oats in the bucket. He looked straight at me, and I could almost see the thoughts cascading through his horse brain, 'oats or freedom?'

Then I stood still, and he came towards me, his ears pricked. He walked straight up to me and plunged his muzzle in the bucket of oats. I slowly put my hand up and got hold of the lead, clutching it very tightly, so no matter what I wasn't going to let him go.

"Thank you! Thank you!" I said to the heavens above.

"That's orright, missus!"

"He's a right 'andsome 'orse!"

"Canna pat 'im"

"Yes, yes, of course, but pat him on the shoulder."

As soon as each of the young boys solemnly patted Balius's shoulder, I quickly reloaded him. I didn't want to risk him escaping again. The boys were a jolly bunch, and they asked me about a hundred questions. I shared my biscuits with them and thanked them profusely for their help, and then I leapt back into the driving seat to travel on. There was no way I was going to let Balius out of the trailer again – not until we were in the safe enclosure of Ned Sperrit's yard!

The adrenaline had been coursing around my body, and it took ages to subside. I drove on, and on, and on and then I felt tiredness sweeping over me. I pulled over into a layby and half-filled a bucket of water and offered it to Balius. He dipped his muzzle in but wouldn't drink, 'you can take a horse to water' or in this case 'take water to a horse'. I climbed back into the driver's seat and lay down across it and shut my eyes for a quick power nap. I woke up feeling very disorientated. I must have been asleep for at least an hour.

Flustered I started up the Land Rover again and pulled out and drove on. It was almost dark before I finally got to Preston. I drove around and around for half an hour before I found Ned's yard. At least this time I recognised the entrance to the narrow alleyway.

At the gates, I called, "Ned! Ned!" and he opened up, and I could see his merry little eyes crinkling in the headlight lamps. I very nearly flung my arms around him and kissed him, but restrained myself in time, in case he misinterpreted the gesture.

"Oh, Ned! I can't tell you what a drive, all the way from Dartmoor to here! But I can't wait to see Copperplate."

"Aye, lass, all in good time, let's get this big chap sorted out first," he said in his funny northern drawl.

I was feverish with excitement now. The hard slog of driving all day had disappeared like mist in the sunlight, and I was on tenterhooks to see the animal that I was sure would be my new horse. I had an instinctive feeling that she would be the one.

Chapter Eleven – Meeting Copperplate

I led Balius to the stable indicated by Ned, and all the time, I was looking around for a chestnut head hanging over a stable door. The other horses were all looking at Balius, checking out the newcomer. Then I saw her, in the stable right next to Balius. She had a beautiful delicate face with the unmistakeable dish of an Arabian mare and a muzzle that could fit in a teacup.

"This is her!" I said to Ned.

"Aye lass, that is Copperplate."

I patted her, and I imagined that I felt a deep connection. Whereas Balius was such a boy with his calm intelligence, she was very feminine, sweet and docile.

"She's an Arab?" I said.

"She's only three-quarters, but from the Crabbet line, bred by Lady Wentworth, which is not as Araby as the Egyptian Arabs."

"What is the other quarter?"

"Well that I'm not sure of, could be anything."

"Would you mind bringing her out, so I can see her?" I asked.

He slipped through the door and put a headcollar on her and lead her out. She was quite light-boned, four white socks and a crooked blaze down her face. She was wearing a warm stable blanket, and I lifted it to see the white splash on her belly. I ran my hand across her side and could feel her ribs, and her bony haunches.

"I love her markings!" I exclaimed.

"Well, I was right about her, she did belong to Ophelia Nettlebed. She rode her for three years, showing, show jumping, and did some horse trials in the pony club. She was a grand little mare, and Ophelia certainly clocked up some wins. She was sold to a small stud who wanted to breed show stock but slipped her foals twice and was sold on. I'm not sure how but she went through a number of sale rings and ended up at the bottom of the heap. It was lucky I spotted her. I've been feeding her up, and you can see she's picked up, a bit of a sheen on her coat, and I've had the lad up on her, just quiet riding around the streets to start to build up her muscle again, and he loves riding her, goes like a dream he says."

"That sounds good, but I was kind of hoping that I might have something with a bit more open experience."

"I know that Ophelia was a little goer and she did jump her in some open classes, and they were always in the money. It's a bit unusual for an Arab to be much at jumping, but I guess she's the exception to prove the rule."

"Will I be able to try her tomorrow?" I asked.

"Yes, of course, there's a bit of a yard you can ride around, but no fancy arenas like you'll find at Mark Lansdowne's."

I frowned, just the mention of Mark's name set my back up. He was the king-size blot on the landscape at Blainstock.

"He should be down at Badminton at the moment," I said.

"Yes, that's a fiasco for sure, the weather you know, it's being run as a one-day event, so he's not going down in the history books this year, even if he won!"

"Really, he will be disappointed," I said a little smugly, my better self not triumphing.

"He's not the only one," said Ned grimly. "Now come on in, don't worry. I always come out last thing to check they're alright."

Ned's sister was as grumpy as she had been on the last visit. She plonked down corn beef hash in front of us, and the white sauce was lumpy and the onion under-cooked, but I didn't care, I was starving, and it had been a very long day. I sat there chewing on the crunchy onion and gulping down the lumps in the sauce, dreaming of jumping the mare around the open jumping at one of the big shows, perhaps Richmond, or even Harringay. If she had a good jump in her and had the speed around the corners, then we'd blitz the jump-offs. I went up to the guest bedroom, which smelt distinctly musty, with a sheen of dust on the heavy wooden furniture, but I was oblivious, dreaming of a string of red rosettes and a mantelpiece groaning with silver trophies.

I woke the next morning, and the rain had arrived up north. Streams of water were pouring down the bedroom window. My heart sank to my boots, how was I going to try her in weather like this.

"Don't worry lass," said Ned in his comforting wise old voice. "I've got a mate with an indoor arena. We'll put her in the trailer and take her over there. You'll get a good try on her, and he's got some jumps as well, so you can put her over some poles."

"Ned, you are a miracle-worker!" I said. Then I remembered I didn't even know how much she cost. Hesitantly I asked him.

"We'll see how she goes with you lass, the better you go, the higher price I'll ask," he said, with a cunning smile.

I gulped at this. I was not at all experienced in horse-dealing and negotiation, I guess if I was clever, I would make sure that she didn't look her best today, but I was just not that type of person.

After lumpy porridge improved only with lashings of brown sugar and cream, we went down to the stables. Ned went along and checked every one of the horses, and the lad kept mucking out. I went and looked over the half doors of Balius and Copperplate.

"Do you think we could take Balius as well if it's not asking too much? He needs some work after yesterday's long journey," I asked.

"Sure, he can come along for the ride, me mate won't mind," said Ned.

I loaded Balius first on the right-hand side, and I was so proud of him, the way he quietly walked up the ramp. Copperplate was probably determined to show how much she was worth and walked on quietly and stood beside him.

"There they love each other already," said Ned as if he were a matchmaker. Ned directed me through a maze of grey streets with not a glimpse of green. I was so glad that I didn't live here in this urban landscape, so grim and depressing. Finally, we drew up at a driveway with a sign saying, "Manchester Riding School". We drove down, and Ned directed me to sweep around and pull up on the far side.

I unloaded the horses and led them under a roofed area where they could be tied up and then I got my tack for Copperplate. She was much narrower than Balius and shorter in the back, and I realised that his saddle was not a good fit. It looked like I would need four new saddles if I bought her.

Balius was stamping his feet, and I dived back into the Land Rover and pulled out his canvas rug, so he didn't catch a chill. Ned led the mare into the large indoor riding school. It was set up with jumps that stood at a good three foot six, and I realised that I was going to have to jump a horse I'd never ridden before. It was going to be a challenge. I'd always thought it took months to get to know a horse to be able to ride it properly. Now, I was going to have to step up and presume she was well-schooled then I would just ride my heart out and we would see how we went!

I mounted her and sat still in the saddle. She stood quietly and obediently. I closed my legs around her, and she stepped forward. I maintained a light contact on her mouth, and we walked around the arena twice. Then I pushed her on to a trot. She had a very light step, not as powerful and strong as Balius. Everything about her was feminine and delicate, and it made me feel a bit like a blundering elephant. I rode her across the diagonal and gave her the aids to canter on the right leg, and she answered immediately. Ned was right; she certainly had been well-schooled. I pushed her into her bridle and asked for a little more collection. I felt her drop her haunches, lift her head and flex at the poll. She knew exactly what to do. I cantered once around the arena on the right leg. Then I attempted a little extension at the trot across the diagonal, and then we struck off on the left leg. She was an absolute delight!

I cantered three times around on the left, then back down to a trot. I circled the jumps and decided we could pop over the smallest one that only looked about three feet high. I pulled up and shortened my stirrups two holes then I rearranged myself into a jumping position. I remembered what Linda had told me, upright position on the approach then bending forward as we rose into the air over the jump.

I hoped that I would be able to 'see a stride' into the fence and I lightly pushed her on, one, two, three and we were a little too far away, but she leapt forward and stretched her neck out, and I gave her enough rein, and we were over. I took back contact and then I went for the double; the first element was three feet six and two short strides and over the second element, which looked more like four feet. She was perfect, and certainly knew what she was doing, and tried her hardest to please. I was in love. I just had to buy her. Now I had to ask how much.

I rode back to Ned, who was chatting to his mate, both smoking roll-up cigarettes.

"Well, what do you think?" he asked.

"She's lovely. How old did you say?" I asked.

"Rising fourteen this year," he said.

"And are there papers for being part-bred Arab?"

"No, they got lost along the way."

"So how much?" I asked.

Ned looked at me speculatively, no doubt thinking that I had a very well-off stepfather.

"How about eight hundred."

I did some quick mental calculations. I had only £720 in all, assuming that Richard came through with the half that he had promised.

"I haven't got that much," I said a little crestfallen. "You know she is rising fourteen years old, and no papers, and she's not yet in peak condition.

"You drive a 'ard bargain," said Ned. "Well seein' as you are such a good 'ome, I could drop it down to £700."

"What about £650," I said with a cheeky grin.

"Well let's meet in the middle £675, but you drive a 'ard bargain you do!" They both laughed merrily, and I wondered whether I couldn't have talked him down a bit more.

"I can pay you £340 in cash now and then Richard will send you a cheque," I said, hoping desperately that this was going to be alright.

"I think I can trust Richard," said Ned.

I jumped off, and we shook hands on the deal. I had just bought myself a second horse, and I was absolutely thrilled. She was not what I had at first envisaged, but was an absolute darling, and I couldn't wait to load her in the trailer and drive her home.

"Now you untack her and throw a rug on her so she doan' get a chill and then give that big grey chap a spin. You never know I might make you an offer you can't refuse!"

I went to open my mouth and protest that I would never sell him, but then I saw he was joking.

"I might just put those jumps down a bit if you don't mind and I can try him over them," I said, feeling as if I were riding a wave of success and up for anything.

"We'll put them down," said Ned, tipping his hat at me.

"Low as low can be," I said. "He's just starting out."

I went out to swap the saddles over. I felt as if I were floating on a fluffy white cloud in a cerulean-blue sky. It was one of those moments when you feel that life holds every promise, and nothing can ever go wrong again.

I mounted Balius inside the arena, and he felt very bouncy. I guessed that yesterday's long journey, not to mention his escapade in the park and this strange new arena were making him feel decidedly unsettled. I trotted him around, rising lightly so that he could warm up.

After about fifteen minutes, he settled a little, and I pushed him into a working canter. Twice around in both directions and then I gave him lots of space and rode him towards the first jump. It was only two feet high, and he saw it, threw his head in the air and tried to rush. I turned him three strides away and rode him in a small circle until he settled again then I rode him towards the jump, and he popped over without a problem. Then I pushed him into a strong canter around the outside edge, and we flew over the double without hesitation. I pulled him back to a walk and gave him a very loose rein and let him walk around calmly.

"Is that all lassie?" asked Ned.

"Aye," I said. "We'll quit while the going is good."

"He's got promise, that big chap, don't suppose you want to sell him?" asked Ned's friend.

"Not in a million years!" I exclaimed and rode him out.

We loaded them back into the trailer and went back to Ned's. I rang Richard to confirm that he would pay the other half of the cost for Copperplate then counted out the notes for Ned. He wrote me out a receipt which detailed Copperplate's particulars and the fact that an amount would still be paid by Richard Micheldever. There was still a long grey afternoon ahead of me, and I was tempted to set out for Scotland this afternoon. But I decided it would be better to get an early start. I asked Ned if I could be of assistance to him in the stables as I wished to thank him for his hospitality. He smiled at this suggestion but told me it was a pleasure to have me as a guest. I settled down at the kitchen table with a mug of tea and a packet of gingernut biscuits and decided to peruse his magazines.

I found many articles of great interest and spent a very pleasurable afternoon reading about the great and the good and imagining my own photo with Copperplate and Balius starring in various equestrian competitions. I was still undecided about whether I should continue to focus on showing and show jumping or whether I should try my hand at eventing, or perhaps dressage.

Em was trudging around the house sniffing loudly, and I wondered whether this wasn't an indication that she found me a nuisance. I was tempted to offer to dust the living room, but then I thought this would be rude as if implying that it certainly needed dusting! On balance, I decided it would be more polite not to offer, which suited me very well. I did help her to cook dinner and together we managed to concoct a spaghetti bolognaise that was not particularly delicious but at least edible. I did the washing up afterwards then went out to see my two horses. I took down a list of what Ned had been feeding Copperplate and patted her and told her what a lovely beautiful mare she was and we were going to live in the Scottish Highlands. Then I slipped back through the yard and took some magazines up to my dusty bedroom, setting the alarm for very early in the morning.

Chapter Twelve – Driving North

The drive back up to the castle was uneventful, and I certainly didn't try and unload my precious cargo along the way. I had learnt that lesson. Mummy and Richard came rushing out to see me when I got back and 'oohed' and 'aahed' over Copperplate and fed her and Balius pieces of apple. Richard insisted that he would see them settled in their stables and I went inside with Mummy and talked nineteen to the dozen filling her in on all my adventures. Although I must admit, I kept quiet about the dog smuggling.

I was up at break of dawn the next day and ran out to the stables. I wanted to see Copperplate again. I was worried that I had been seduced by Ned's horse dealer charm and perhaps had imagined that she was as wonderful as I thought. She seemed to have settled in well and whiffled away at me as if she knew me already. I ran my hand across her ribs, and she wasn't that skinny, she would soon fatten up. John came around with the morning feeds at which point she was more interested in what he was tipping into her manger. I forgave her this.

I went back inside for breakfast, luxuriating in the wonderful cooking at the castle. After weeks of Bryony's toast and tea, this was truly delicious. Cook had prepared kedgeree, which was one of my absolute favourites.

"Now, Jill, you must remember it is your birthday next week," said Mummy.

"Oh yes, it is," I said. I was not as excited as I usually was when my birthday was looming. To be eighteen years old was rather frightening. I wasn't sure that I wanted to move into adulthood. That is if you counted eighteen as being an adult, rather than the traditional twenty-one. Going up to open classes in horse shows was hard enough.

"We thought we might buy you two saddles," said Richard.

"The trouble is that I need four saddles," I said apologetically.

"Oh, Jill! This is not like you at all," said Mummy.

"No, it's not that. It's just that Balius is much longer in the back, and broader with not much wither, whereas Copperplate is more petite and will need a narrower fitting."

"Yes, that is a perfectly valid point," said Richard, patting Mummy's hand. "With horses, there is always something else that you need."

"What if I get the saddles for Copperplate," I said. "And I can continue to ride Balius in the one I've been using. It'll be some time before he's competing and by then I may have raised some more money."

"Excellent. I know a very good saddler who can come out and take some measurements of both you and the mare, and he can have them made up in a few weeks.

"We thought we might have a little celebration up here. What do you think?" asked Mummy.

"But I don't have any friends," I said plaintively. "Except perhaps Linda, we could ask her, and John and Hugh from the stable yard, but beyond that there's no-one." I was rather appalled to find myself saying this; it sounded pathetic.

"Yes, I see the issue," said Richard.

"What about Ann-Marie? Perhaps she can come up and visit and then we can just have a jolly little family celebration, go out for a slap-up meal at a restaurant."

"I'm not sure what Ann-Marie is up to, it seems as if her life is a nonstop whirl of social occasions, tripping from Paris to London and back again."

"I'll ring her mother and enquire," said Mummy firmly. "No matter what it's going to be a wonderful birthday for you."

I dashed out to the stables then as I was planning on riding Copperplate in the arena. Fortunately, Mark was still away at water-logged Badminton. I was very excited and nervous. I mounted, and we walked around quietly. I tried to feel her, divine her spirit, understand her personality. Obviously, it would take time. We walked for at least ten minutes, and I practised walk and then halt. Then I tried rein back, which she did without a problem. For years I had been teaching children to ride, and we had always focused on walking, halting, and rein back. Then I thought perhaps a turn on the forehand.

Copperplate was perfect with everything. This was certainly the trained horse that I wanted. I gave her aids to trot, and after a few circles, I aimed for some collection, true collection, the way that Linda had taught me. Copperplate responded well. An Arab's head carriage is naturally high, but she bent at the poll and accepted the bit. I was thrilled but again cautious. I didn't want to overdo it on her first day. I took her back outside, and we walked down the road and trotted back. Several cars passed, and she didn't give them a second glance. I could see now that she was going to be my perfect horse. Back in the stable, I untacked and rubbed her down. Then I threw a light canvas rug on and let her go in one of the fields. She seemed quite happy and put her head down to eat the new spring grass. I leant on the gate and watched her. There is nothing more satisfying than to lean on a gate and watch one's own horse grazing.

I went back and saddled up Balius. He had jumped well in the arena at Preston, and now his training was to begin in earnest. I was struck by how different he was to Copperplate in every way. She was feminine and delicate, and he was strong and masculine. Her stride was measured, light and balanced, and he had so much scope but still needed to establish balance and rhythm. We started off with walking and trotting then I jumped off and set up the cavallettis. We would do that exercise that Linda had shown me.

Soon we were swinging over the poles with a beautiful rounded stride. He lowered his head, and I could feel him getting the rhythm. Then I jumped off again, and I put a very small jump one stride beyond the grid, so we trotted down, then one trot stride and over the last fence. He tried to canter off as he landed, but I brought him back to the trot. If we approached at the trot, then I expected him to trot on landing.

Afterwards, I tried cantering some small circles, keeping his balance and cadence, pushing him into a semblance of collection. It was hard work, and by the time we had finished our session, I felt as if my legs were chewed string. This was so much more exhausting than just careering around the moorland, enjoying the fresh air and swooping and sweeping like the kestrels above.

After I'd rubbed him down, I let Balius go with Copperplate. I was hoping that they were going to be best friends. Again, I leaned against the gate and watched them. Balius trotted around the perimeter of the field as if to check that nothing had changed in his absence. Then he went over to Copperplate and dropped his head to graze next to her. I thought how lucky I was, two such amazing horses and all my life ahead of me.

I went back to the castle, deep in thought. I was thinking that I might draw up a proper training schedule, but, first, I needed to take Copperplate down to Linda's and see what she thought of my new mare. Linda would have some good ideas about what we needed to do.

Mummy told me that Ann-Marie was coming up next week and was going to stay a whole six weeks.

"That is abso-bally-lutely fantastic!" I cried. I couldn't wait. We could do so many things together, especially now with my two fantastic horses and I was hoping to talk her into going on the Merrivale's pony trek with me.

"Is she not continuing with her social thing?" I asked.

"No, apparently, she's rather tired of the endless round of cocktail parties and dances so her mother thought that six weeks of bracing Scottish air would do her a power of good. I'm sure you can think of all sorts of things you can do together."

That afternoon the saddler was coming at three o'clock, so I went out and caught Copperplate and brought her in. I was awfully excited about this. I'd never had bespoke saddles made for me.

The next day Linda watched me riding Copperplate around her arena. She studied us very seriously and didn't say a word.

"Come on, tell me how great she is," I said light-heartedly.

"She's certainly well-trained and got good paces."

"Do I hear a big 'but' coming up?" I asked, suddenly wondering if there was something seriously wrong that I had missed entirely.

"No, not at all, she is everything you said, and I don't want to rain on your parade."

"But???"

"She seems a little stiff in the back, not swinging through as freely as she should."

"I haven't noticed anything like that," I said.

"No, well, you're not watching her intently with my critical eye," she replied. "But that's what you pay me for."

"What is the answer, what do we do?" I asked anxiously.

"In Germany, they do quite a lot of what you might call physiotherapy. It's just starting up, these ideas of manipulating the horse in certain ways. I can show you a few moves. I think it might be losing the foals and then going down in the world. We don't know what happened to her. But with some manipulation and lots of exercises that work on her flexibility. I'm sure she'll be back to normal soon."

I had never heard about physiotherapy for horses, but it certainly made sense. I was so lucky to have Linda up here in the back of beyond, she was like a European coach and probably a thousand times better than that weird little ferrety man who came over and helped Mark.

After we finished with a jump over a small course of just two feet high but with different distances that required lengthening or shortening strides, I dismounted. I took the saddle off, and Linda showed me how to lift up her legs and move them around in different directions. Then taking her head and pushing it back towards her shoulder, massaging her along certain lines, in particular along the line of the shoulder where it met her neck.

"Can you feel the difference after a little massage, you can see her relaxing?" asked Linda.

I wasn't sure that I could, but I had huge faith in Linda. I took a scrap of paper and made notes for myself, so I wouldn't forget.

I continued to work with the horses every day and then went down to have a shorthand lesson with Miss Square, who was amazed at how much my speeds had improved. I told her that I thought we should really concentrate on my German at the moment. We arranged a new schedule of two lessons a week, and my life in Scotland carried on full of plans and hopes.

Then Ann-Marie was arriving on the afternoon train, so Hugh showed me how to harness Bonnie to the trap so that I could meet her at the station in the same rather astounding style in which Mummy and I had been greeted when we had first arrived. It was such a quaint and charming move, and I was longing to see my friend's astonished face.

Ann-Marie stepped off the train, and I jumped up and down to get her attention. Not that I needed to as there was only the two of us on the platform. I grabbed one of her suitcases and groaned dramatically.

"What have you got in here, we'll need to hire the carrier," I said.

"You, funky monkey!" she exclaimed when she saw the pony and trap.

"Russian rabbits! Back to you!" I said. We laughed uproariously. It was the same as it had always been with us. We plunged into a frothing sauce of delicious gossip about our mutual friends. I had told her about Malevolent Mark, but she had always looked a little puzzled at this. She had read about him and thought he looked dashing and handsome.

We got to the castle, and I was delighted to see her mouth drop open as if she were catching flies.

"Oh Jillikins, this is just too gorgeous. I don't believe it!"

"I told you it was a castle!"

"But I mean this is a real castle!"

"Not a pretend one," I replied sardonically.

Mummy came out to greet us and hugged Ann-Marie warmly.

"Oh, I am so glad you could come and stay, poor Jill is a bit lonely up here."

"I am not," I replied stoutly. "You make me sound like Billy No Mates."

"No. of course not," said Mummy soothingly.

"I just can't believe it, utterly stupendous!" said Ann-Marie. "And are there animals' heads hanging on the wall, and suits of armour standing in the corners? Oh, turrets!" she said, clasping her hands together.

"Well, at least you don't get to meet a long line of old retainers here in the courtyard!" said Mummy, laughing. "Come in, come in, we have a ceremonial bowl of chicken broth for you. It is a custom that travellers are always fortified with home-made chicken broth."

"Oh, my goodness, please tell me it won't have giblets floating in it," said Ann-Marie.

We sat down to supper. We indulged in a stream of gossip about our buddies from Chatton. Then we had to hear all about Ann-Marie's recent stint in Paris working as an *au pair* and enjoying a glamorous lifestyle with her French friend, who she had met at finishing school in Switzerland.

"Tomorrow we're going riding, and you can have your choice - Balius my big grey youngster or Copperplate my darling little chestnut mare who is perfectly trained and sweet as apple pie."

"I can't decide," she said. "Perhaps we should toss for it."

In the end, Ann-Marie decided that she would like to ride Balius, never having ridden anything over 16.2 hh before.

Chapter Thirteen – The Golden Eagles' Nest

Ann-Marie was mounted on Balius, and I was happy to ride Copperplate. John came with us. He had promised that he had something to show us, but he wouldn't say what until we had ridden away from the stables. He was riding one of Mark's horses, a big black gelding that was at least two inches taller than Balius.

"I've found a golden eagle nest, it's about five miles ride up along the loch aways," he told us.

"That sounds amazing," I replied. "Don't you think Ann-Marie?"

We rode on. Then I turned to John.

"Why is it such a secret?" I asked.

"It's just that the eagles prey on the red grouse sometimes, and they can get shot, and I love them, I would hate that to happen. I've been watching them for a while now. They also pick up lambs as well."

I nodded wisely as if I totally understood, but I'm not sure that I really did. Who would shoot them? Surely not the men employed to watch over the red grouse? I decided that I would just keep quiet, not ask too many questions. After the dog-smuggling incident, I had been thinking very hard about the rights of animals and what was right and wrong, and I found that the more I thought about it, the more complicated it became, and my head hurt. But I knew it was important. I had always thought of myself as a horsey person, but this had to extend to being in favour of being kind to all animals.

But it just wasn't that simple. I had been appalled at David Staley rapping the showjumpers, but now I found out that many professionals used this method. Pure logic had to tell you that it wasn't right. Perhaps if I got it all straight in my mind, then I could have a career as some sort of advocate for animals and their rights? Now that would be more exciting than taking down shorthand and typing up documents! But it would probably entail some sort of training in legal issues. I wasn't sure that I wanted to go on with further study. Especially now I had a home with every possible horse luxury available to me!

"Will we get to see the golden eagles?" asked Ann-Marie, jolting me out of my state of abstraction over the rights and wrongs of the treatment of animals.

"No, they're not there at the moment, if they were we shouldn't go disturbing them. But I do see them a lot up here."

"What do they look like?" I asked.

"They're most amazing, not quite as big as the sea eagle but they have a beautiful golden colour. Their nests are huge round circles of woven twigs and branches and full of the bones and corpses of their kills."

"Oohhh," said Ann-Marie in affected tones.

"I remember them talking about a Lord, you know a Peer of the Realm living in his own eagle's nest," I said slowly.

"That sounds really odd," said Ann-Marie.

"I can't remember what they were saying. It was at Christmas dinner with the Lansdownes."

We fell silent and enjoyed the open air. It was the first time that Ann-Marie had ridden over the estate and she was taking in all the gorgeous vistas and then we could see the loch in the distance, shimmering, with a broad path of golden sunlight sparkling across the surface. We trotted until we came to the loch and rode on the path around it. John led the way, and we went on towards the hills that towered above us. We followed a tiny path that wound between thickets of dead brown gorse, along a track that was rarely used. As we got higher up the wind blew in from the sea, cold gusts of icy air. The top of a crag was towering over us. The going was very steep, and we leant right forward and took a tight grasp of the horses' manes, or we would slip off over their tails.

Finally, we came to a ledge. We were very high up. The loch seemed small below us. The air up here was so fresh and clear you felt like you could reach out and touch it. John said we should dismount. He suggested that one of us hold the horses and he would take the other one up through the rocks to a place where we could look across and see the nest without getting too close.

I offered to let Ann-Marie go first. She clambered over the rocks behind John. The horses stood quietly, and I tried not to look down and imagine tumbling down the steep slope to the bottom. Mark's black eventing horse and Balius were far too big for this type of mountain climbing that was more suited to goats. We wouldn't be doing this again.

"Oh, Jill, it's absolutely flipping fantastic!" said Ann-Marie as she skidded back down the hill.

I almost opened my mouth and said, 'don't say flipping', then shut up.

"OK, you hold the reins, and I'll have a look," I said impatiently.

I climbed up behind John. It was hard work, looking for handholds.

"Just move one leg or one arm at a time, then you always have three points of contact," he said to me.

"Alright, alright," I replied testily. But I was just being tetchy. If one of us fell, it would be John who would get the blame. We reached the top, and I saw the nest. It looked messy, a random pile of small branches and twigs, but it was cunningly tucked into a cleft in the rock, much bigger than I had imagined, and I could see the bleached white bones of dead animals, and even what seemed to be a little lamb's skull.

"Wow, this is very special," I said in a whisper. Although there was no sign of the eagles themselves, I spoke softly.

"They'll be back soon, and then they'll lay their eggs," said John. "Then we wouldn't want to risk coming near it.

"I wouldn't want to be attacked by a protective eagle, those talons and the beak look pretty scary."

"Aye," said John. "Come on, let's go back. You won't say anything, will you?"

"No, no, cross my heart, and I'll tell Ann-Marie not to say anything as well."

It was very awkward riding the horses down the steep and narrow path, and at one stage Mark's big black horse stumbled and a shower of small rocks scattered down the mountain slope. I hated to think what Mark would do to John if his precious horse, undoubtedly worth several thousand pounds, was to have an accident and fall down the hillside.

We made it back to the trail around the loch and trotted steadily back to the castle.

"You are lucky Jill, to be living up here in this splendid countryside, with two brilliant horses. I love Balius, but he is rather a challenge after our dependable ponies."

"Yes, you're right," I said. "But the winter was a bit grue, very dark and dismal."

"Yes, I must admit. I have come to like the bright lights. Paris was divine, you know, and the French food was utterly delicious."

I thought about this for a while. Was I missing out on a sparkling social life up here in the Highlands, living in almost splendid isolation. I had always loved the countryside, but my childhood version of the country consisted of little roads with grassy verges, small patches of woodland and commons on which to canter. This was so much bigger, majestic mountains looking down over sweeps of empty moorland.

"You know that Linda went to Germany as a working pupil in a dressage stable," I said. "I thought that I might like that. What do you think?"

"I don't know," said Ann-Marie, screwing up her nose. "I imagine it would be hard work, and those German dressage horses are utterly massive."

"Let's canter up here," said John, "it's getting late, and I've got to be back for lunch."

"Us too," I said, and we cantered up the slope. Copperplate as usual tucked in behind the others, perfectly quiet and obedient. Balius responded to the big black gelding and tried to race.

"Stop! Stop!" shouted Ann-Marie. "I'm sorry it just felt like he was going to take off, I'm not used to such a big strong horse."

John slowed down ahead of her. I hadn't really noticed before, but he was a very good rider. He seemed to effortlessly control the big eventing horse. I wondered whether he also had ambitions to compete, be more than just a groom. I wondered where he had learnt to ride like that, perhaps he had a natural talent and had seen enough of Mark training his horses to pick up ideas about the correct aids.

I was starving and looking forward to lunch. I still hadn't got over the ghastly food I had been subjected to in Cornwall. Cook at the castle was brilliant at producing hearty meals. Today was a mutton stew flavoured with mint, with fluffy mashed potato and small buttered green peas.

"You know Mark is back from Badminton. I've invited the Lansdownes over for dinner tonight, so it's a chance to introduce Ann-Marie and hear all about what happened at the horse trials. I understand it was a disaster weather-wise."

Ann-Marie perked up at this. Her eyes were sparkling, and I remembered how she had admired the photo of Mark in *Horse and Hound*. Inwardly I groaned, I hated Mark and dreaded having to sit down in the same room as him.

"What are you and Ann-Marie going to do this afternoon?" asked Mummy, who knew only too well how I felt about Mark, even if she didn't know exactly why. I had never told her that he had called her a fortune-hunter.

"I thought we might take the dogs out and I wanted to show Ann-Marie the cross-country course."

"That sounds fun," said Ann-Marie smiling happily. "I love those huge dogs. They're like Baskerville hounds!"

We spent an hour or two walking around the course and talking about different lines that we could take. Then we threw sticks for the dogs and tried to train them to jump over the fallen logs.

"Copperplate is a very accomplished jumper, isn't she?" asked Ann-Marie.

"Yes."

"You could try her tomorrow over these jumps."

"Yes, I could," I said. I didn't say what I was thinking. I was a little nervous about these big solid jumps. Although I was quite happy showjumping, knowing that if we hit a pole, it would fall. If we hit one of these jumps, then it was solid, and the horse and I would come a cropper.

"Let's think of a course for you, and I can watch you tomorrow," said Ann-Marie, not at all in tune with my silent fears.

"I thought I might practise more in the arena with her, perhaps tomorrow just the banks and a few logs. I've got to start jumping Balius in the arena as well."

Ann-Marie looked a little puzzled, but she didn't comment. We walked back down to the stables, and all Mark's eventers were there but luckily no sign of him. We walked around and looked at each of the horses, then went up to the field and caught Balius and Copperplate and led them down to their loose boxes.

We were walking back to the castle when Mark zoomed in, driving his natty little sportscar. He had his girlfriend, Diana with him, her perfectly styled smooth blond hair tucked under a silk scarf and wearing a fur coat. Her makeup was perfect, and her thin lips were outlined in bright pink.

"Oh look, Jill has been out riding her pony," said Diana in tinkling ice-cold tones.

As Balius was 16.2 hh plus and Copperplate at least 15.3 hh, this was hardly true, and it reminded me of an absolutely horrid girl, Susan Pyke, who throughout my childhood had delighted in making patronising and supercilious remarks. I ground my teeth.

"Let me introduce my friend Ann-Marie," I said in stilted tones. "This is Mark Lansdowne and Diana Barton-Tompkin."

"Oh hello," gushed Ann-Marie, as I had guessed, she had been rather keen on the idea of Mark.

"Diana, I do believe that you are one of Yvonne Dufour chums. I spent a lot of time with Yvonne in Paris, such a hoot!" said Ann-Marie in quite a different voice, her vowels all rounded.

I was utterly stunned. I couldn't work out whether Ann-Marie was playing these gruesome twosome at their own game, or whether she was claiming acquaintanceship in the way she had been taught at finishing school in Switzerland.

At least it had a rather satisfying effect upon Diana, who looked rather disgruntled. She didn't know where to go with this, undoubtedly assuming that my best friend would be of the same lowly birth as she imagined I was. At least, Ann-Marie had some understanding of *noblesse oblige*, the weird rating system, who was 'one of our kind' and who was of a lower class.

"It is so wonderful to finally meet you," said Ann-Marie fluttering her eyelashes at Mark in a film star type of way, which was another thing she must have learnt at finishing school, how to catch a husband.

"How do you do," said Mark, not at all put out. He was used to this type of reaction from women.

Diana then dragged Mark off. She was huffing and puffing, undid her headscarf and was flipping her hair around in that way that girls do when they want to attract attention from men.

"Well, that squashed her!" said Ann-Marie. I looked at her. Nonplussed. I wasn't quite sure what to make of this. I didn't think I could bear to ask Ann-Marie what she really thought of Mark. I didn't want to have to come to terms with what she might tell me.

"Come along, Jillikins," said Ann-Marie giggling. "Don't worry, you and me against the world."

This slightly reassured me, but I did feel we were on rocky ground.

"Tomorrow, let's go down to Linda's riding school. We could both have a lesson. If you don't mind, I would like to try Copperplate," said Ann-Marie. "I am just dying of jealousy, you have two of the most wonderful horses, and I don't have a single one."

"But what are you going to do?" I asked. I couldn't see Ann-Marie's future at all. It seemed like a desert without any horses.

"Well, would you be hugely surprised if I was to tell you that I'm secretly engaged?" said Ann-Marie.

"Yes, utterly gobsmacked!"

"Well, I am, and it's not to a nob like Mark Lansdowne. My fiancé is utterly divine and get this, he is an MFH – Master of Foxhounds."

"Wowee," I said. After all, if one did have to get married then a MFH was the absolute dream of all time for horsey girls of our generation.

"You see, I will have horses in my future. In fact, Percy has got stables full of them."

I had about a million questions that I wanted to ask, but I couldn't get one single word out.

"We just have to wait until Percy gets a divorce from his wife, Maud," said Ann-Marie with a deadpan face. Then she began to laugh and laugh, "Gotcha! Gotcha! A good one!"

I managed a hollow laugh, but it was a bit too close to the knuckle for me. But if we could pass it all off as a joke, then that would be alright. After all, I had had my secret little dream of marrying Horatio, even if it was solely for the purpose of irritating Mark.

"Come on! Let's ring up Linda and book a lesson tomorrow. That is if you don't mind me riding Copperplate."

"No, of course not," I said stoutly. It wasn't the first time that Ann-Marie had ridden one of my horses, and I certainly hoped it wouldn't be the last.

"Tell me when are you going to take her to a show and enter the Grade C and the Open Jumping?"

"I've been looking through the events listed in *Horse and Hound,* and I saw that there was a show in three weeks near Inverness. It's rather a long drive, but I thought it might be fun. I've asked the Secretary to send me a schedule, and I'm hoping it will arrive tomorrow. Will you still be here in three weeks' time? You could come and cheer us on," I said.

"I've got a much better idea. Didn't you tell me that Linda has a most amazing ex-racehorse called Joe. Why don't you ask her to go with us, then she would have a chance at competing?"

"That is so thoughtful of you," I said realising what a selfish pig I had been. I hadn't given Linda's situation a thought. She didn't even have a car, let alone a Land Rover and a horse trailer.

"We could have a marvellous time, a real adventure like when we were kids," said Ann-Marie. "You two can slave away with the horses, and I'll lounge in the marquee and stuff myself with cream teas."

"I'll ring her now to book in the lessons. Then we can ask her. Hopefully, the schedule will arrive in the morning post before we set off."

That night I slept in the camp bed which we had set up in my turret bedroom. As a guest Ann-Marie had the rather grand bed. My best friend was utterly enraptured with my bedroom, and she was determined to explore every square inch of the castle.

The dinner with the Lansdownes went better than I had envisaged. Mark was showing off and talking about all the famous people he knew who had been riding at Badminton, but that was fascinating. Ann-Marie listened with great attention, no doubt storing up the anecdotes as future currency in her society conversations. I was also memorising every detail for the great day when I also would be rubbing shoulders with such equestrian stars. It made me all the more determined to ride and train and also be competing in that world.

The next morning, I rode Balius, and Ann-Marie rode Copperplate. We walked down to the village.

"Can we just trot a little? So, I can get the feel of her," said Ann-Marie.

"Of course," I said, relieved that Balius felt just the same as normal and had not suffered any bad effects after he had had another rider the day before. I felt a little ashamed at these ignoble fears. I had never doubted Ann-Marie's riding ability in the past. She had actually learnt to ride before me and had been quite accomplished when I was a mere beginner when we were twelve years old. We had always competed against each other, and often she had done better than me with her pony who knew how to present himself well in showing classes.

We arrived at the riding school, and suddenly, I was seeing it through Ann-Marie's eyes, the way things look different when you have visitors, and it did look rather homely. The stables were converted outhouses of different types, the yard was swept clean, but the cement was cracked, and there was only a small arena with a thin layer of sand to reduce the concussion on the horses' legs.

However, Linda's knowledge and ability as a teacher were unsurpassed, She had the knack of seeing just where improvement was needed and had seemingly countless ideas for exercises and techniques to improve both one's riding and the way that the horse went. I introduced Ann-Marie, and she smiled in a jolly and friendly fashion and didn't seem to be turning her nose up at the rather ordinary facilities.

Linda had us going around the arena within minutes, and then I forgot about my silly doubts and concentrated on riding. I was also fascinated to see Copperplate ridden by someone else, so I could learn more about the way that she moved. I had to admit that Ann-Marie rode her very well, pushing her up into her bridle. We practised extension today which was something that Balius hadn't done before. At first, he just went faster, but Copperplate had obviously been so well-trained, swishing around at a beautifully expressive extended trot, pointing her hoofs like a ballerina's toes. I wasn't sure that I would have managed so well with her.

"I'm afraid this arena is a little small for teaching extension. It's a matter of the horse carrying its head a little lower than during collection, and concentrating on the driving force of the hindquarters, rather than a lifting effect which is important in collection."

Linda watched our efforts for several minutes.

"I think Jill that we might do better to try this in the arena at Blainstock which is twice the size of this one. But you did get a few good strides in that last attempt. Perhaps we should stop now. I thought you might like to try some jumps."

She dragged a couple of wings over and set up some poles.

"I haven't seen Copperplate jump yet, but you told me that you jumped her before you bought her, Jill?" she queried.

"Yes, that's right," I said.

"We'll just trot over in the beginning," said Linda. "As Balius is such a novice."

I was watching Ann on Copperplate, and my mare really didn't want to trot as if to say that was for babies and beginners. She cantered and jumped neatly. I trotted Balius in a circle and then aimed him at the jumps, he did an awkward elongated trot stride over the first and then rushed on over the next.

"Take Balius over again, don't come out of a trot until he does it perfectly," said Linda.

I took him over three times. Finally, he seemed to understand what was wanted.

"Now let Copperplate give him a lead, and you canter over," said Linda.

He was much better at the canter, and his smooth jumping style melted back into a steady canter as we landed.

"Do you want to try Copperplate over something higher?" asked Linda, looking at Ann-Marie and then at me, not sure who was making the decisions.

"I don't mind if you want to," I said shrugging.

"Yes, rather," said Ann-Marie enthusiastically.

"I'll help," I said slithering down from Balius and taking the reins over his head and giving them to Ann-Marie.

"I have only got enough poles and wings for three jumps," said Linda apologetically. "How high do you want to jump her?"

"I took her over three feet six and a bit higher on the day I tried her," I said uncertainly. "She is an experienced jumper."

"And I can see that Ann-Marie is also experienced," said Linda.

We put the double up to three feet six and then built another jump on the other side of the arena at four feet. I took back Balius's reins and took him outside of the arena to give Ann-Marie more room.

She cantered around twice, looking at the double and then as she turned the top corner gave the aids and Copperplate flew over the first element, two regular strides in the middle and over the second element. Ann-Marie sat lightly in the saddle, giving her enough rein then taking it back again as she landed, down and around and then they went towards the bigger jump and Copperplate went over it with a perfectly judged stride.

"One, two, three," I counted as I watched. She really was a lovely mare, with a flawless style.

"Do you want to jump Copperplate, Jill?" asked Linda.

"No, no," I said, a little too emphatically. Linda looked at me, and I could see the question hovering in the air, but she decided not to ask it, then nodded.

"I think that is the end of the lesson," she said, glancing down at her watch.

"Jill and I have had a wonderful idea," said Ann-Marie. "We were wondering if you would like to bring your horse, Joe, isn't it? We're planning to go to a horse show near Inverness in three weeks. We can take the two horses in the trailer, and the camping equipment and Jill will take Copperplate of course."

"Oh!" said Linda, clearly thrown by this idea. However, Ann-Marie's good-hearted enthusiasm carried her along.

"What about the riding school?" she asked. "The horses?"

"There must be someone who could come in and hold the fort. Jill and I helped to run our local riding school, and it was a high point of our young lives. We learnt so much, and we had some rather exciting adventures. Well, perhaps you don't want adventures, but don't you have some pony-mad pupils who could step into the breach?"

"I suppose I could ask Louisa, she is very responsible and keen, and could bring along her friend Bobby," Linda said thoughtfully.

"That's it!" said Ann-Marie with such conviction that it was settled.

Over lunch, we pored over the schedule and talked about which classes to enter. Richard was so sane and sensible about these matters. He proffered his opinions, and Ann-Marie sat there with her mouth open in wonder and surprise.

"You are a proper horsey person!" she said to him. He smiled at her with a twinkle in his eye. "Gosh, you are a lucky duck having Richard to talk to," said Ann-Marie.

We decided that I would ride Copperplate in the Ladies Jumping class and the Open.

After lunch, we walked the dogs back down to the village and on to the riding school. We found Linda cleaning tack, and we sat down to help her. It was just as it had been when Ann-Marie and I had helped Wendy at Mrs Darcy's riding school. Linda decided that she would also enter the Ladies Jumping and the Open Jumping.

The next morning there was no evasion possible. I had to begin to jump Copperplate. But I procrastinated. I insisted that Balius needed to at least master the rudiments of extension. I rode him around the arena until Ann-Marie confirmed that we had managed a few good strides. Then I came up with the bright idea of practising self-carriage. Where, for a few strides, one pushed forward one's hands and allowed the horse to maintain his own balance and rhythm. I was determined that I would always ride with the lightest of hands and contact, not relying on pulling Balius into a semblance of collection, but rather achieving the true mastery of getting him 'on the bit'.

After this, I declared that I was exhausted and insisted that Ann-Marie rode Copperplate. I set up the jumps at very easy distances, regular strides between each. Copperplate jumped flawlessly, neatly tucking up her legs and adjusting her own stride so that she took off at the right point. I decided to see how she went over the wider jumps, and I set up an oxer which was four feet wide and three feet high.

"You need to let her have plenty of rein," I told Ann-Marie, suddenly the theoretical side of jumping seemed much easier than performing it myself.

"Yes, I'll make sure I give her a good length of rein," she replied, not resenting my instruction at all.

Copperplate was challenged by the width of fences, but she tried her best and managed it. She had a rather helicopter style of jumping, springing off her elegant hind legs and bouncing up in the air. She would always manage height better than width. I did wonder how she would fare over the very wide tabletop type obstacles in a cross-country, and it confirmed my idea that I might stick to showjumping with her.

"Now, Jill, I absolutely insist that you jump her next. It is you that will be competing on her in slightly less than three weeks," said Ann-Marie in a voice that would brook no argument.

I mounted and did my best to suppress the illogical fear that was hovering around the edges of my consciousness. Copperplate jumped just as well for me as she had for Ann-Marie. She was extremely experienced, and it appeared that she had had many different types of rider in her life. She cleared each jump in a very professional manner. I felt my irrational fears receding a little. Ann-Marie put the jumps up bit by bit, and in the end, we jumped four feet.

"That was a very polished performance," said Ann-Marie and I didn't argue with her. My feelings seemed out of step with what was actually happening, but I said nothing.

"I think she has had enough for today," I said, stroking her neck softly. She really was the sweetest of characters.

We let her and Balius out in the field together, and they seemed to have settled into a happy friendship, cropping the spring grass side by side.

That afternoon we took out Richard's big plain brown horse and Balius's mother, Bonnie, and rode over the hills. Both these horses were natives in the district and so sure-footed that we were able to relax and soak in the scenery. We rode along the loch again and this time circumnavigated it.

"We could take the boat out tomorrow, if the weather holds," I suggested.

"That would be wonderful. I've been asked to go sailing in the south of France later in the summer, so I must hone my nautical skills," said Ann-Marie, as if it were the most natural thing in the world to go sailing in the Mediterranean. I couldn't decide whether or not I would like to be living Ann-Marie's life. I had never really thought about travelling, and it did seem to hold some allure. On the other hand, if you have horses, you can't just flit from here to there as they are a full-time occupation and can't be backed into the shed and left there until one returned.

On the following day, Richard suggested that we take the fourteen-foot wooden sailboat out and he and Mummy came with us and taught us how to manage the sails. I found it confusing at first, but Ann-Marie took to it like a duck to water. I always seemed to be half a step behind and threw myself from one side of the boat to the other as we changed direction, which I had now learned was called 'tacking'. Although I must admit, it *was* rather fun to feel ourselves skimming across the surface of the water which glittered with the sunshine.

My new saddles arrived the day before my birthday, and we rushed down and tried them on Copperplate. They fitted her perfectly, and I sat in them, and they felt divine as if they were moulded to my body. I knew that this was going to improve my riding tremendously. After the initial fitting, we sat down and rubbed them with warmed neatsfoot oil, working on them until the leather darkened evenly.

My birthday was celebrated with an excursion out to a restaurant about twenty miles away. It was rather grand, and we dressed up. I wore my beautiful long dark green velvet dress and Mummy lent me some long gloves, and we pinned my hair up. Ann-Marie used some rather subtle, but effective eye shadow on my lids and it did give my eyes the appearance of being much larger. Ann-Marie was looking extremely elegant and sophisticated in a sort of shimmering silver sheath which matched her long dark tresses. Her hair had always been a rather jolly bright red, but now she must be doing something to it as it had mysteriously turned into a glossy chestnut brown. She wore a glittering necklace that matched her earrings.

"We do look very grown-up, don't we?" she giggled as we sat in the back of the car. I felt like a doll all dressed up, but as we tucked into a most delicious meal, I forgot about my appearance and concentrated on the food. The meal was utterly divine, fabulous French cooking in the depths of the Scottish Highlands. It was a lovely evening, and I was happy to spend it with my very nearest and dearest.

Ann-Marie gave me a lovely card with a very sophisticated pastiche design.

"I've arranged your present, and it should arrive tomorrow," she said in mysterious tones.

I had no idea what it might be, so you can imagine my astonishment when I woke up the next morning to find Ann-Marie looking out the curved window that looked down over the castle courtyard.

"Your present has arrived," she said, turning around to smile the biggest widest smile.

"It must be big to be in the courtyard!" I exclaimed.

"It is that!" she said, laughing fit to burst.

There in the centre of the courtyard was Ann-Marie's horse box with a huge pink ribbon wrapped around it and a banner saying, "Happy Birthday Jill"!

"Your horse box! I don't believe it! That's far too much, how can I accept that?"

"Don't be silly, we've hardly used it in recent years, and it's an old model so it's not worth selling and it will help you with your equestrian career. We can take it to the horse show near Inverness!"

I threw on my dressing gown and rushed down the staircase and out into the courtyard. Of course, It wasn't the first time I had seen the horse box as occasionally Ann-Marie's mother would allow the groom to drive us to gymkhanas or shows that were not within hacking distance. It was large enough for three big horses, or perhaps four smaller ponies and the area that overhung the cabin was used for storage, or one could put a mattress up there to sleep. We had never slept in it as our events as children were only for a day.

"That is just too supersonic for words!" I said. "I cannot believe you would give me such an amazing present!"

It was as if I were in one of Mummy's children's storybooks where the heroine is showered with good fortune at the end of the story. Now I had two horses, two brand new saddles and a horse box! What more could any human being wish for!!

Ann-Marie was looking rather smug. All my doubts about her since she had become rather worldly fell away, and I knew that she was the best friend anyone could ever wish for. There was nothing wrong with moving into new worlds and having new experiences, she was going one way and me another. There was no reason that we couldn't maintain a happy friendship as we made different life choices. I had one of those rather rare moments in life when I saw that everything was as it should be.

Chapter Fourteen – The Horse Show

We were embarking on our journey to the horse show the day before so that the horses could adjust to their new environment. As we now had room in the truck, we decided to take Balius as well so that he could experience an event with lots of other horses in preparation for the day when he would make his competitive debut. At this rate, no young horse was ever going to receive such thorough training to prepare him for a competitive life!

The day of our departure dawned sunny with the promise of warmth, a cloudless blue sky and a very soft breeze that brought down the scent of early blossoming heather.

"This is such a heavenly place I will come back whenever I have to recover from my frantic social life," said Ann-Marie smiling mischievously. I think she had divined my uneasiness over her new life and was teasing me.

John drove us down to Linda's, where we were to pick up her and Joe. Then she would drive from there as she was an experienced horse box driver. She had a mound of gear stacked up in the yard, and Joe was bandaged up with a smart travelling rug.

"Yoohoo!" carolled Ann-Marie as we drove into the yard. She was in cackling high spirits, and it was infectious. We pulled down the ramp and loaded Joe. John helped to stash Linda's gear, and then we all piled into the front seat. John wished us good luck and waved as we drove away. He looked as if he would have liked to be coming too.

Ann-Marie and I sang as we drove along and soon Linda was joining in. She had a beautiful contralto voice, far more musical than Ann-Marie or myself. We drove for two hours, stopping once for fuel and then another hour, and we arrived at the event. There were signs posted along the last mile, and we wound our way along narrow country roads and then drove into the estate called Druim Uaine – what a tongue-twister! We rumbled down a long driveway lined by elm trees just coming into leaf. The vista of green fields of carefully tended turf with showground bunting, a carousel and other carnival rides, three roped arenas and various tents and pavilions was fantastic.

I just loved that moment of arrival at a competition. The sense that anything was possible, all the hopes and excitement, gleaming horses their shining bits and stirrup irons flashing in the sunlight, the smell of fresh turf crushed under steel horseshoes, and riders concentrating on their last-minute training.

"Oh! Look at that house, isn't it splendid!" exclaimed Ann-Marie. Up on the hill was a rather impressive two-storey house, the windows glittered in the sunlight, and the gardens were well-kept, topiary trimmed in the most extraordinary bird shapes.

"Do you know the people that live there?" I asked facetiously.

"No, not at all, perhaps we will meet them this weekend," she replied hopefully.

Linda made a small noise in her throat, and I suspected that she was making a negative judgement about what she might have perceived as shameless social-climbing. I felt that I should defend my best friend. I chose to believe that Ann-Marie simply had a zest for life and new experiences.

We soon forgot about these tricky social questions. We drove to the stable yard and talked to the Secretary of the event who directed us to our stables. The loose boxes were spacious, spotlessly clean, situated in a large stable yard with wooden boxes brimming with flowering spring blossoms. Other competitors had arrived, and their horses were installed, hanging over the stable doors watching attentively, neighing and whickering and moving around. Copperplate looked a little anxious. Perhaps she was remembering the way she had been passed from one person to another and thought she might be in a sale yard. I hoped she wasn't going to have a bad reaction, uncertain of her future. Joe was tittupping around, perhaps remembering his racing days. Balius, the inexperienced young horse, was the most sensible, looking around intelligently but without a sign of stress. Again, I felt that stab of conviction that he was going to be a most amazing horse.

After we had settled them in their loose boxes, we drove to the area where we could set up camp. We had two small tents, and we had great fun erecting them. It became obvious that none of us had ever been a girl guide! It was wonderful having our own little camp, and we arranged our tack in the truck so that it would be easy to find. Then we went over and fetched the horses from their stables and saddled up to ride them around. There was a cross-country course here which was used for three-day events, and it had been opened up for competitors, but we were not meant to do any of the jumps.

We rode out, a merry trio, and the horses were happy with each other. We walked for at least fifteen minutes letting the horses warm up slowly, then trotted and cantered up and down the undulating countryside looking at each jump and discussing how we would tackle it if we were to jump around the cross-country. Linda was a mine of information and Ann-Marie, and I drank it up, finding her technical know-how utterly fascinating.

We put the horses back in their stables and gave them their evening feeds, topped up their hay nets and buckets of water. There was a great deal of bustle and movement around the stables, and we surreptitiously looked out for famous people that we had seen in *Horse and Hound*.

"Look over there, it's Sheila Willcox!" hissed Ann-Marie.

I looked where she was pointing, of course, I had heard of the famous Sheila Willcox, who had won an unprecedented three Badmintons in a row and a gold medal at the European Championships in Italy. She was very tall with beautiful blonde hair, set perfectly and subtle makeup. She was known as a glamour girl. She strode around like an Amazon warrior, but we didn't recognise her horse, it wasn't High and Mighty. We knew that she was a regular competitor in Working Hunter classes and show jumping competitions. Perhaps she had brought one of her novices. I wondered if I might find myself competing against her in the showjumping the next day.

That evening back at the camp, we cooked sausages and heated up baked beans in a saucepan. The other competitors were friendly and called jolly greetings to us as they walked around. The Ladies Jumping class was scheduled for eleven o'clock, so this meant we didn't have to be up at the crack of dawn. We sat around our little campfire, and different competitors drifted over and chatted to us. This was the life that I dreamed of, living in a horse box and travelling from show to show. I was so excited that I was sure I wouldn't sleep a wink. But the excitement of the day must have tired me out, and I found that I slept soundly through the night and was awakened by the sound of Linda making tea. Ann-Marie, who was never a natural early riser, rolled over and groaned. We wouldn't bother with breakfast until after we had mucked out the stables and given the horses their first feed of the day.

It was another beautiful day, and I hoped that this was an auspicious beginning to my career of competing in adult classes. We gulped down our tea and set off for the stables. The horses were pleased to see us and tucked into their feeds as soon as they were tipped into the mangers.

"What time will we saddle up to warm them up?" asked Ann-Marie.

"I thought ten o'clock, and walk around for at least quarter of an hour. I don't think that Copperplate will need as much riding in as Joe," said Linda. "He always thinks that he's back on the racecourse."

"Let's get back for breakfast," I said. "We need some food to sustain us through the day."

We tucked into bacon and eggs and fried bread, and in the open air, it tasted even more delicious. Then we brought the horses over to the truck and tied

them up and tacked up. Ann-Marie was going to ride Balius around with us, sitting on him to watch from the ringside. Joe was very excited, and this seemed to upset Copperplate. When I mounted her, she was a bit fizzy, and I found my previous fears rushed back in with a vengeance. This was different from any pre-event nervousness that I'd experienced in the past; it felt very weird. I told the others that I was going to ride off by myself. I made sure I was in my correct position, but I felt very insecure as if I would slide out of the saddle at any minute. I forced myself to trot and felt all unbalanced. I tried to relax and think about other things and pushed on to a canter. Gradually, I felt better and went over to the collecting ring and jumped the practice jump a couple of times. Copperplate was faultless, meeting it on the correct stride and clearing it easily. Ann-Marie rode over on Balius and offered to hold Copperplate's reins while I walked the course with Linda.

Walking around with Linda was brilliant, like having my own personal coach who supported me not only in training but also at competitions. The Ladies Jumping was a big deal, hotly contested by a host of women, both glamorous, hard-bitten, local and from further afield. I tried to concentrate on the jumps and not get distracted by the other competitors walking the course.

There were a dozen obstacles, and each of them was at least four feet high. The fourth jump was the triple, and it stretched to at least eight feet wide. I reminded myself that for a wide jump, we needed plenty of pace and impulsion. Linda pointed out that it was a tight corner to the left then only three strides to the triple. She suggested that I swing out wide around the corner, so I had at least four strides to pick up the pace before the triple, then back to a bouncing stride for the red brick wall which looked at least five feet. I was drawn to jump twentieth, and Linda was tenth, so I would have time to watch her and Joe. I felt totally dithery with nerves and tried to take long, deep breaths to steady myself.

I walked Copperplate around and around the collecting ring and watched the other competitors. Not one of the first nine went clear, and then it was Linda. She sat perfectly still, in a correct position. Joe was excited and pulling, snorting and prancing sideways, but she didn't seem fazed. The bell went, and they cantered around the arena, taking almost a full minute before they went through the start, and by then Linda had Joe balanced and moving forward in a straight line.

The pair of them looked very impressive. Linda was thin with long brown hair that she wore in a single plait down her back. She sat so straight in the saddle, bending elegantly over the jumps and back in the saddle within one stride. They cleared the first three jumps perfectly and then in spite of the

advice that she had given me she turned at the corner giving herself only two strides to the triple. Joe soared over it with inches to spare, and the crowd clapped spontaneously. Linda brought him back to a very collected bouncing stride, and they helicoptered over the wall, and then they flew over the final seven obstacles. It was the first clear round, and to my eyes, it appeared flawless. I dropped Copperplate's reins and clapped vigorously.

"Well done! That was absolutely fabulous!" I called as she rode past, her cheeks bright pink with effort.

"Thanks, Jill," she said, almost shyly.

Then I trotted a few circles and popped over the practice jump twice. Copperplate felt very reliable and steady, especially compared to the fiery Joe. I knew that it was up to me; she could easily go clear as long as I rode her properly. I pulled myself together, and I was determined to ride to the very best of my ability.

The competitor before us also rode clear. So that was two clear rounds, and I was determined to be the third. Copperplate was cantering, her head raised a little, so she could look towards the jumps and gauge their height. The bell rang, and unlike Linda, I cantered only a small circle and then through the start. Copperplate was perfect. She met every jump on the right stride. I took the corner wide and giving her a little extra rein I pushed her on and over the triple. I felt her stretch her neck, and we cleared it, then I sat down in the saddle and collected her for the wall. Again, she cleared it. We didn't look like hitting a jump, and we went clear. The spectators clapped, and I patted her neck enthusiastically. It was everything I hoped for. There were a few more competitors but no more clear rounds so we had to be at least third and I felt that this would be our proper place as both Linda and the other rider who jumped a clear round were miles better than me.

"Jill, you can do it," said Ann-Marie fiercely, her hand on my shoulder. Balius turned around and nudged my boot as if to tell me to be courageous.

The stewards went and widened the triple and put each of the bars up six inches, and then the wall had an extra layer of bricks, another six inches and the last fence was a sharp turn to the left after the wall was an oxer which was raised another six inches and widened another foot. The loudspeaker announced that the jump-off would consist of only four fences; number one the brush, number two the triple, number three the wall and number four the oxer. We didn't have another chance to walk the course and had to

envisage it ourselves. I was to go first, the pathfinder, so I had no idea whether to go all out to go quickly or to go carefully to make sure I had no poles down. I decided that I would aim for a clear round rather than the fastest. Joe and Linda were always going to be faster than us, and I imagined that with a slow clear, we would be a very creditable third.

Copperplate cantered into the ring with a tiny shake of her head as if to assure me not to worry. The bell rang, and we cantered smartly through the start. My chestnut mare seemed to know what she was doing, and we set off for the first jump at a brisk pace, over and clear, and then we approached the triple at a slight angle so that we could fit in four paces, and I made sure to give her plenty of rein. She pecked slightly on landing, and I fumbled the reins and then she was heading for the wall at a pace that felt much too fast, over it and I had got myself together again, and we galloped towards the oxer. Copperplate adjusted her own stride, met it at a perfect distance, and we were over clear. I leaned forward and urged her on to gallop through the finish.

"Bravo, bravo!" shouted Ann-Marie. "That was absolutely super, Jill! Well done you!"

"That was good," said Linda smiling as she cantered past me into the ring.

I pulled up next to Ann-Marie still mounted on Balius, and we watched Linda. Joe seemed to have settled now. They cantered a small circle and then through the start, going very, very fast. I held my breath thinking that perhaps Joe might flatten too much and not clear the jumps. Over the first and then she swung him around on his haunches so that rather go around the long way they were approaching the triple with just one stride. He cleared it without any effort and then she collected him a little for the wall, which he cleared and then flat out to the oxer which they soared over and then through the finish as if they were winning a steeplechase.

Ann-Marie and I were shouting with excitement at the top of our voices, and Linda ducked her head, looking embarrassed at our enthusiasm. She was four seconds faster than me. Then she joined us, and we watched without a word as the third competitor went around. She would have to go very, very fast to beat Linda but she knocked a single brick out of the wall, so was relegated to third.

We were called into the arena, and Linda stood at the head of the line, a very worthy winner. Copperplate and I were second, and I was more than conscious that it was due to my brave little mare rather than my own ability. The woman who came third congratulated us both and asked Linda if Joe was for sale. Linda shook her head, hesitantly. Then we galloped around the arena in a victory lap with Linda holding a very handsome silver cup in the

air. Our winnings were rather impressive and would more than cover the cost of our fuel and stable rent and food, so we were laughing all the way back to the camp. I was determined that I would put a few pounds aside, to save up for Balius's new saddles.

Ann-Marie helped us to unsaddle our horses, rub them down and throw light rugs over them. A few sips of water and a handful of oats each and then she walked them around while Linda and I drank some lemonade to give ourselves energy. The Open Jumping was scheduled for three o'clock in the afternoon, so we had a couple of hours before saddling up again. We took the horses back to their loose boxes and then treated ourselves to a meal in the marquee. Linda and I were both reliving our rounds, jumping in our heads. Ann-Marie, however, was looking around, bright as a blackbird. We lined up and ordered our meals and carried them over to a table.

"Isn't that a famous show jumper over there?" hissed Ann-Marie in a stage whisper. I looked over, and it did look like a familiar face, but I couldn't think who it was. Linda had her head down eating. She didn't look up.

"Aren't you pleased with your Joe?" asked Ann-Marie.

"Yes, of course," she replied. "If he goes as well in the Open class then he really has proved himself."

I wondered why Linda wasn't brimming with high spirits, on top of the world after such a convincing win. Then I remembered how the other competitor had asked her if Joe was for sale. Perhaps Linda was short of money and felt torn, wondering if she shouldn't sell her amazing horse. I frowned a little at Ann-Marie to shut her up.

"I was thinking, we could have entered Balius in the Novice Hack," said Ann-Marie, chattering on.

"Next time, if you like," I said. "You're welcome to ride him."

"I didn't bring up my riding kit, but hopefully we'll be able to travel around to lots of shows, now that you've got the horse box. You'll have to learn to drive it yourself, Jill."

"That's on my list of things to do," I replied.

We finished our meal and drifted over to the stables to check on the horses. There were plenty of comings and goings, and we hung around looking at the other horses and riders. Then we led Joe and Copperplate back to the truck to saddle up ready for the Open Jumping.

"Surely the jumps won't be much higher than this morning?" I asked Linda anxiously.

"I don't know, I'm not sure," said Linda. "You shouldn't be nervous, you're very good, and Copperplate is so reliable and well-trained, you'll be fine."

"I think you'll win again," I said humbly.

"It's bad luck to say things like that," she retorted.

The horses were saddled, and we mounted and walked over to the collecting ring. The course was being rebuilt in a new design. When they called the competitors in to walk the course, Ann-Marie took the reins of the horses for us. Linda strode ahead in silence, and I thought she was annoyed with me. I tagged along behind pacing out distances between the jumps that seemed even higher than those of the morning. This time there were fourteen obstacles which included two doubles. I puzzled over it for a while, with Copperplate's short stride, I wondered whether I shouldn't try for three strides. I felt desperately inexperienced and fought the temptation to run after Linda and ask her to help me. The second double was three short strides between the elements. The brick wall was still included and was the sixth jump, and a water jump had been constructed, which was at least eight feet wide. I hoped that Copperplate had jumped water before.

I was the third to jump, which was even scarier. I wouldn't be able to watch the others and see how they went. I quickly trotted and cantered some circles to warm up Copperplate and try to calm my frazzled nerves. If it was my chosen career to be a showjumper, then I would have to become more confident or else I might as well spend my remaining years sitting in front of a typewriter.

I jumped over the practice jump three times, and each time Copperplate cleared it without a problem. The first two riders clocked up four faults each, and both times it was at the wall which was just two strides off a rather tight corner. I decided to take the long way around and hope that I could make up the time and not incur time faults.

I rode in and saluted the judges and cantered in a wide circle waiting for the bell. Then I cantered through the start, my stomach feeling as if it was filled with madly thrashing butterflies. I pointed Copperplate at the first jump and in my nervousness, I kept her on too tight a rein, she just clipped it with her hind hoof, and I heard it clatter to the ground. Somehow this made me feel much better, we just had to get around the course, and we wouldn't be in the jump-off. I pushed her on and released my tight hold on her mouth. She gave a little toss of her head as if to say, 'just leave it to me' and we went over the second and third jumps without a problem. When I got to the first double with the rather long two strides between the elements, I decided to leave it up to Copperplate and sat her lightly. She lengthened her stride

without a problem, and we cleared both. The wall was next, and I steered her out on a wide curve so that she had plenty of run-up to it and we cleared it, then over the next double again with lengthened strides, and then on to the finish.

"Four faults," announced the loudspeaker. I patted her neck. It certainly wasn't down to her that we hadn't gone clear. I became very conscious that I was going to need considerable experience with these bigger courses before I could expect to be winning. I thought that the morning's second was a fluke.

"Well done you!" said Ann-Marie. "You know you look really professional out there Jill, it won't be long, and you'll always be in the money."

I grimaced at her and dismounted with relief. I had jumped enough today, and I was secretly glad that I wasn't going to be in the jump-off. We watched the other competitors. They went through one after the other, some with three refusals and elimination, others with four faults, or eight faults and then it was Linda. Her face was very pale, and her mouth set in a straight line.

"She doesn't look very happy," said Ann-Marie.

"Watch this horse here, he's very promising, I'm going to make an offer on him," said a voice behind us. I looked around and saw that it was the woman who had come third in the Ladies Jumping class this morning. I felt dismayed for Linda, what an awful decision she was going to have to make. We watched them fly around clear, which meant that at this point, they were winning. However, her clear round seemed to set a higher standard, and there were three further clear rounds.

So, there were four of them to jump off, and I was totally relieved that those of us with four faults weren't going to have to go into the ring again. This time the competition was very stiff, and Linda was going to have to fly. The five jumps in the jump-off were put up to at least five feet, and they looked absolutely enormous to me. Linda was the first to go, and she simply flew around, but, unfortunately, Joe knocked the second element of the double. This meant that her competitors could be more careful and not go flat out, and, in the end, she came third.

She rode in with the other horses, and when she was presented with her third rosette and her envelope with the winnings, we shouted and cheered like mad. She looked over to us and gave us a funny little twisted smile.

"She doesn't look at all happy," said Ann-Marie.

We waited for her to finish her victory lap and then congratulated her heartily. She dismounted, and we walked back towards the truck. When we got there, the woman who had come third that morning caught up with us.

"Can I speak with you?" she asked politely.

"I'll take Joe and untack him for you," said Ann-Marie.

We left her there in deep conversation with the woman, and I feared the worst. She would have to agree to sell Joe if she was offered enough money. We got back and attended to the horses, throwing rugs over them and tying them up with water and hay nets. We waited and waited, and, eventually, Linda returned.

"I'm selling Joe, they're taking him immediately," she said her voice breaking.

"Oh no, that is too bad," said Ann-Marie.

"I have no choice," said Linda, "I wasn't born with a silver spoon in my mouth."

"I might take Copperplate back to the stables," I said tactfully, shooting Ann-Marie a meaningful look that meant 'shut up'.

We walked off and left Linda to say goodbye to her precious horse.

"Just be careful what you say," I said. "I don't think the riding school is the most profitable business in the world and I don't suppose she has much choice."

"I see," said Ann-Marie.

After putting Copperplate away and checking on Balius, we walked slowly back to the horse box. Joe had gone, and Linda was packing up our gear.

"I assume we're leaving quite early in the morning," she said.

"As soon as we're up and have had breakfast," I replied.

"I forgot to tell you we've been invited to the big house tonight for a drinks party. It doesn't matter if we don't have cocktail dresses, they said to just come as we are," said Ann-Marie brightly. Linda shot her a look and stalked off.

"Oh no, I don't know what to say," wailed Ann-Marie.

"There is nothing we can say," I replied. "I don't imagine she'll come with us tonight."

But I was wrong. Linda appeared with her makeup applied and clean slacks and a white shirt, and she looked extremely elegant. I gasped when I saw Ann-Marie's outfit, a rather tight, short bright orange skirt and a matching top in orange and white stripes.

"You look rather ... ," I just couldn't think of the right word.

"Groovy, is the word that you're looking for," said Ann-Marie smiling at my evident shock. "Really Jill, don't be such a square. What are you wearing?"

"Well, strangely enough, I didn't pack my party outfit," I said in a voice loaded with irony. I had to make do with a clean pair of jodhpurs and a white shirt.

"Let me do your makeup for you," said Ann-Marie, flourishing her mascara brush at me.

"No, thank you," I said with as much dignity as I could muster.

We set off for the party, Ann-Marie leading the way in her outfit which I could only assume was the height of fashion in swinging London, Linda looking rather glamorous with her long legs and hair brushed out and me looking like a child in jodhpurs, at least I had long black boots. My hair was frizzing out everywhere after wearing a riding hat all day.

At the party Ann-Marie and I watched Linda working the room, chatting to other guests, laughing and gesticulating with her hands. Ann-Marie then set out to enjoy her evening, chattering blithely to everyone. It was me who was the social dunce. I found myself talking about Copperplate and Balius until the other guests' eyes glazed over, and they would slide away. It was not just open jumping classes, but also grownup parties at which I had to improve my skills!

The party went on into the night, and we left at midnight, crawling into our tents and falling asleep with exhaustion. The next morning, Linda was the first up, boiling the kettle over the campfire. She brought us mugs of tea.

"Breakfast in bed in a tent," said Ann-Marie.

"I guess we need to make an early start, I have to get back and check on my ponies and horses at home," said Linda.

By the time we crawled out of the tent, the campsite was almost packed away, and Balius and Copperplate were standing tied to the truck wearing their travelling bandages. Nearly everyone else had left, and we loaded the horses, and we were on the road, roaring back to Blainstock. Ann-Marie had partied too hard the night before and went to sleep on the back seat.

"I wanted to ask you a favour," said Linda quietly. She almost looked embarrassed.

"Of course," I replied.

"Would you mind if we took the horse box down to Cheshire next week, there are two horses there that I've been asked to train. It's not finally settled yet. I have to go down there and ride them, and if we reach an agreement, then I'll take them back to Scotland and train them for three months."

"Wow!" I exclaimed. "They're paying you?"

"Of course, I'm not going to do it for nothing," said Linda, shortly.

"Well, of course you can take the horse box if you want, or I'll come with you, I'd love to come. Where is it that we have to go? Whose horses are they?"

"It's a young woman who is studying at university, and she wants her horses trained during her last term, doing her finals. Her name is Elspeth Crashaw. She's actually very nice. I remember meeting her once. I was talking to her father last night, he'd seen me jumping Joe, and he was rather impressed."

"So, it means that something good has come out of this, having to sell Joe," I said.

"Yes, you see I'm a professional, or at least trying to be, and I can't live on a few riding lessons and trekking in the summer. I have to prove myself in competition, and I'm not going to be able to afford to compete properly on my own horses, it's always going to be riding other people's."

"Yes, I can see that. When you think of everything that Mark has laid on, and he's done nothing for it," I said bitterly.

"Mark was always going to have it easy. But life isn't like that for everyone. Quite frankly I wouldn't want to be Mark, imagine living inside that swollen head of his!"

"Yes, you're right," I said. "I do admire you. You work so hard."

There was a moment's silence. Then I added.

"I would love to come with you. I like visiting other horse people and seeing how they train their horses. I feel like I'm learning things all the time."

"Jolly good," said Linda, trying to lighten the mood, "and I'll pay you back with free lessons."

"Whizzo," I said, realising that this was a brilliant idea, and it also meant that in the future I could go to shows with Linda, helping her with the use of the horse box and inestimably beneficial for me in terms of her good advice. It was a situation which would benefit both of us.

We arrived back at Blainstock, with our rosettes displayed on the dashboard. John was the first to congratulate us, and then Mummy and Richard came over too, clapping their hands with delight, at our success. They invited Linda to come in for lunch and then they could hear all our news.

We sat around the table, and I felt so happy. This really was our new home now, and Linda and I would team up, and we could go around the shows. Ann-Marie would be back to her social whirl, but she was still my best friend, and that would never change.

THE END

Printed in Great Britain
by Amazon